The Break

Tales from a Revolution: Nova-Scotia

The Break

Lars D. H. Hedbor

Brief Candle
Press

Cover art: Detail from illustration "Dartmouth Shore in the Harbor of Halifax," by Joseph F. W. Des Barres, 1777. Reproduction courtesy of the Norman B. Leventhal Map Center at the Boston Public Library.
Interior illustration: A view of the town & harbour of Halifax, from Dartmouth shore, Des Barres, 1781. Reproduction courtesy of the Library of Congress Geography and Map Division.
Cover and book design: Brief Candle Press

Fonts:
Bookman Old Style
IM FELL English
IM FELL Great Primer PRO

First Brief Candle Press edition published 2014
www.briefcandlepress.com

ISBN: 978-0-9894410-8-7

Dedication

To my six daughters and three sisters,
with gratitude for the insights

Chapter I

S usannah clutched the railing of the rickety-feeling ship as it plunged through what seemed to her the worst storm she'd ever witnessed. She allowed as that she might not have that much perspective on the nature of storms at sea; though she had grown up in sight of the ocean, this was her first venture out onto its broad—and at the moment, roiled—face.

She felt ill, and could not discern for certain whether it was the motion of the deck under her feet or the situation that had placed her here that was the cause for the unsettled feeling in her belly.

Clamping her jaw shut, she peered out through the windswept mist, looking for and finding the sliver of shoreline visible along the horizon. It slid by just perceptibly, though it consisted entirely of undifferentiated forest, unbroken by any friendly seaside village or settlement.

Turning to look across the deck at the open ocean beyond, she was glad to see no pinprick of white that might represent an unfriendly sail. Though her father had assured her that the rebels would not make so bold as to attack a merchant ship, she had come to distrust all assurances of stability and safety.

She could not grasp what, exactly, animated the rebels' enmity toward the King, having only a dim awareness that affairs between the Crown and Colonies had been edging toward a disaster for almost as long as she could remember.

It seemed like only yesterday that she had crept out of her room one evening to hear her father and some of his friends discussing in urgent tones the latest outrages of the agitators against Parliament's acts.

A bottle of sack wine stood open upon the table, a lone remainder of a large and satisfying meal. A mostly-empty glass gripped tightly in his hand, a man named Mister Forrester, whom Susannah knew from her trips down to the docks with her father, was speaking, his face red with intensity.

"A perfectly reasonable levy, paying for the King's active and energetic defense of our shores from those French beasts, and they organize to refuse entry to any goods marked with the revenue stamp. What thin sort of gratitude is that, I ask you?"

"I cannot answer for their reasoning," Susannah's father replied. "Gratitude is not in them, I agree, but what's more, they have failed to avail themselves of the normal means of communication with the Crown, choosing instead to engage in riot and disorder to make their unhappiness known."

He shook his head, his face stony in resolve. "It is no wonder that His Majesty has felt the need to respond by sending additional customs agents here to restore us to the orderly practice of properly regulated and paid commerce that obtained before these malcontents began to raise a rabble."

Mister Hawlings, whose trade was not known to Susannah, spoke up now, his tone quiet and dangerous. "They are as small boys, playing with fire in a storehouse because it pleases them to see their shadows leap upon the walls. They will soon discover to their regret that they are not so large as their shadows permit them to believe that they are. Indeed, if they are not careful, they will set these Colonies ablaze, to the ruin of all around them."

Forrester seized upon this point, interjecting, "None will suffer so much as the proprietors of the storehouse—or society—that they so destroy."

His interlocutors nodded, their lips pursed and heads moving in such perfect synchrony that Susannah could not help but giggle at their matched expressions. Her father glanced up sharply in her direction, and she darted back into her room, her heart racing as she heard his step creaking across the floor behind her.

"You are to be abed and resting, not sneaking about, eavesdropping on the private discussions of your elders." His face was no longer comical to behold, but stern and disapproving. She could see at the corners of his eyes, though, a hint of amusement, and she took assurance that she would be forgiven this transgression.

"Yes, Papa," she said quietly, pulling the old blanket that her mother had once used up to her chin and curling up under it meekly.

"I shall ask my friends to keep their voices down, so as not to further disturb your rest, then, and will expect not to see you again until the morning."

"Yes, Papa," she repeated.

Their voices had risen again as the wine in the bottle dropped further, but she had not again succumbed to the temptation to learn what animated their discussion, and could make out no more than small snatches of conversation as she drifted off.

Turning back to the distant shore now, though, she thought that she might have a better understanding of what they had been talking about.

There had come a terrifying afternoon when Forrester had appeared, wild-eyed, at their door, shouting to her father incoherently about tar and feathers, and Susannah grasped after too long that some terrible fate had befallen Hawlings.

The next time she saw the quiet, intense man who had sat at her father's table, he appeared to have been shorn of his hair, and moved stiffly, as though in substantial pain. His intense gaze held a new fire, and the girl was frightened enough to cross the street when she saw him from that time forward.

Too, she had heard talk around the town of a customs boat that had been set afire in an act that some feared would be taken as an act of open rebellion. A pole erected as a rallying point by the rioters was torn down by a group of men—including her father—who counted themselves as loyal to the Crown, despite being confronted with raised fists and angry words from the opponents of the customs service.

Not long after that, Susannah's slumber had been interrupted one night by a commotion outside the house. She heard her father's voice, angry and firm, answered by a jeering catcall. Something had thumped against the side of the house, followed by a sharp yelp from whoever was confronting the master of the house.

Her father had closed the door heavily behind him as he'd retuned inside, and she could hear him stirring restlessly in his bed throughout the remainder of that night. In the morning, though, he volunteered nothing about the incident, and deflected Susannah's questions brusquely.

The most recent confrontation had spurred her father to place them on this ridiculous little ship, pitching across the sea toward a destination as foreign to her as the mythical shores of the Orient, though far closer.

Mister Graham, another of her father's friends had appeared at his step on a dreary morning, looking haggard and disheveled when she opened the door to greet him.

His voice full of weariness, he asked, "Is your father at home?"

"Yes, though he is engaged in his morning ablutions at the moment. Should you like to enter and wait for him?"

"I had better do so, as I know not whether I will be safe in open view."

Susannah frowned at this comment, but stood aside to grant him entry to the house. "I shall go and tell Papa that you await him," she said, a worried expression on her face.

She rushed to the back room of the house, where her father was nearly finished dressing himself for the day.

"Papa, Mister Graham has come to call on you, and waits in the kitchen. He looks very strange and out of sorts, as if something terrible has happened."

Her father looked sharply at her, saying, "You should finish preparing for your lessons with Miss Thayer. You may tell Mister Graham that I will greet him presently."

Susannah did as she was bidden, and though she dutifully tried to attend to the lessons in grammar and diction that Miss Thayer offered, her mind kept wandering back to Mister Graham, and she lost track of what her tutor was saying several times through the morning.

"Susannah, might you spare me your attention,

or are you preoccupied by some event that I ought know of?"

"I am sorry, Miss Thayer," Susannah said solemnly. "I do not know whether I am at liberty to speak of what is troubling me, but I will give you the fullest measure I can of my attention."

The usually kind-eyed tutor gave Susannah a stern look, but the girl's serious expression softened her heart. "Very well. Now, let us go over those declensions again..."

When Susannah returned home, she found her father in a state of high agitation.

"I fear that events have exceeded my ability to justify continuing to expose you to the risk of staying here in our comfortable home, Susannah," he said by way of greeting.

She gasped, "But then where will we go, Papa? Is there some neighbor with whom we must lodge? And what danger urges you to such a conclusion?"

"My compatriot, Mister Graham, lost his home to the action of a mob in the night. They gathered to riot without sometime after midnight, in an attempt to influence him to cease his efforts to defend the Crown from their violence and disorder. In a matter of less than an hour, they had raised themselves to such a fervor that they had fired his house and barn, and this stout servant of the King had no choice but to flee with but the clothing on his back."

His eyes haunted by a fear that Susannah had never before seen, he continued, "I will not stay here and expose you to the whims of the mob as they drag our community into the very flames of the hereafter."

"But, Papa, what of our friends and your business here? Will we leave them with so little notice?" She felt tears begin to form at the edges of her eyes as she thought about her close friend Emma, with whom she had shared confidences and play since before she could remember.

He regarded her seriously, answering, "I would rather that we leave swiftly and leave to Providence the security of our friendships and finances, and take no risk that I should awake one night to find I had failed your mother in her final charge upon me to keep you safe and happy."

He had been unmovable by any number of tears or words, and in a matter of days, they had packed what little they could, and they were crossing from the stability of the land that had cradled Susannah since her birth to the unsteady planks of the ship that now carried them away.

Chapter 2

June the Twenty-Third

My dear Emma,
Our journey to these foreign shores complete, Papa & I have
set to establishing our home here. This task is made more difficult
by far owing to our hasty departure—we were forced to abandon all
but the most treasured of our possessions. Furthermore, we are not
alone in this state, which has resulted in the commonest of household
goods having become both scarce & dear in the shops. We are,
however, making do, & we have in the few weeks of our residency
here conjured a comfortable, though not lavish, domicile. But,
indeed, what kind of domicile we have been reduced to! Emma,
you would never believe that Papa would have taken a place such
as this, but that there are no other choices available. Even so, the
workmen's saws, hammers, chisels & axes make a constant racket
throughout the house as they make it fit for our habitation. It is
difficult to get a decent rest, never mind attending closely to my
tutor. Yes, you read that aright—even among all the privation
of these late events, Papa has secured a new tutor to take Miss
Thayer's place among my daily tasks. He is a youngish man,
quiet & shy to the point of pain, but very learned & quite patient
enough with my inability to attend to his lessons with the necessary
diligence. I do hope that this letter finds you in good health & better

spirits than when we departed, & I will await eagerly your reply. You are my only connexion to the events among all our friends & relations, & I am filled with anticipation of the many intelligences that you will share by return post.

    Affectionately yours,
    Susannah

    The smell of freshly-sawn wood sharp in her nose, Susannah folded and sealed the letter, carefully packed away quill and inkwell in her prized writing box, and sighed for her proper writing desk, abandoned with her old life at home.

    She knew better than to voice any disappointment to her father, though, as it would neither do any good nor improve his melancholy mood. He felt the loss of their fine house as keenly as she, and yet remained utterly convinced that he had done the right thing in quitting the inflamed community, convinced that it was only a matter of time before he suffered the same fate as Hawlings or Graham.

    For the duration of their voyage, he had been uncharacteristically withdrawn and quiet, and the only time that she could get any meaningful response from him was when she asked him about Halifax, where the ship bore them.

    Leaning against the railing on a fine day near the end of the journey, she had asked, "Papa, what are the people of Halifax like?"

    "They are loyal subjects of the King, as are you and I, and they are, I expect, as graceful and well-mannered as anyone we have known in our former home."

    "Are there not rebels there, as well?"

    "No, it is so far removed from the troublemakers in

Boston and Philadelphia that we need not be concerned about the prospects for ill events there." As he spoke, though, Susannah could detect a tinge of evasiveness around his eyes, as though he were speaking these assurances aloud as much to convince himself as her.

He turned away from her, scanning the shoreline as they sailed along it. "What I know of the town is that it was once a place of great importance, when we expelled the French from these shores, but is lately said to be a quieter locale. Indeed, the regular mail packet to Boston was converted to Royal Navy service a few years ago."

Turning back to face Susannah, he said, "I expect that we will find it congenial and relaxed, without either the overwhelming busyness or the acidic rancor to which we have been accustomed." Smiling gently, he continued, "I am not so young as I once was. A bit of quiet sounds good to me, in addition to serving to keep you safe from the hazards of political intrigue and unrest."

Susannah frowned to herself, not meeting her father's steady gaze, and instead focusing on the passing shoreline. The "busyness" that her father now fled included her familiar surroundings, her close friends, and much that she held dear, but had been forced to abandon.

Her father placed his hand on her shoulder, and looking back to him, she saw a sad smile on his face.

"You remind me very much of your mother," he said suddenly, and gave her shoulder a quick squeeze, before dropping his hand. "When she was unhappy with me, she would not say anything to me, but would find something far away to look at."

He sighed. "I understand that you are unhappy

about our departure from the only home you've ever known. All I can ask is that you trust that I put us on the wing out of a clear-headed consideration of the potential for disaster if we remained." Narrowing his eyes as though to shade them from a far brighter light than the sun presented, he added quietly, "I have had too much of loss already in my life to survive any more."

Susannah frowned to herself as she slipped the writing box back into the valise that contained what few precious items she had been able to pack into it in the days following her father's announcement that they were leaving, probably forever. It seemed impossible that he truly understood the losses that he had imposed on her, all in the name of keeping her safe. Why, the trip to this place seemed to hold more hazards than their cozy home and village, even with a few hotheads stirring up trouble. What comparison could there be between unruly young men and the fury of a wind-whipped sea? She shook her head and tried to compose her features before bringing the letter in to her father.

She found him using the kitchen table as a makeshift study. "Papa, could you please dispatch this with the next post? 'Tis but a maintenance of the correspondence I had promised to my dear friend Emma."

Her father looked up from the page that he was perusing and smiled at her. "I shall do so, yes, though I cannot be sure when a post back to home may travel."

She nodded in reply, and paused before leaving the kitchen. "Have you any word as to when we may be able to again purchase flour? I should like very much to practice the baking arts in which Miss Thayer had instructed me, but the bin has been empty for these past several days."

A worried crease forming across his brow, he replied, "No, Susannah, when I spoke to the miller, he told me that he knows not when they might receive some wheat for grinding. He thought that Quebec might send us some barrels of flour, should our local supplies not materialize as usual."

Looking out through the window at a warehouse at the edge of town, he shook his head sadly. When he had spoken with the miller, the man told him that in most years there would be a bustle of commerce there as the harvest came in. Now, though, a single horse and laden cart stood patiently as its driver haggled with the proprietor.

Susannah followed her father's gaze and saw the bleak, rocky landscape past the buildings of the town. Beyond sight, she knew, there were farms being thrown up by yet another shipload of Yorkshiremen, lured here by promises of free land and freedom from game laws and taxes.

While she did not envy them the hard work that they were undertaking to clear and plant the land that they had purchased or had established tenancy upon, she wistfully wished that they had been more inclined to settle in town. She was accustomed to greater opportunities for social interaction than watching an old farmer argue with a merchant.

She sighed heavily and returned to her room, where she sat on her bed and opened the primer that Miss Thayer had pressed into her hands upon her departure. While it was not exciting material, it was better than engaging further in resentful conversation with her father.

For his part, she was certain that he must secretly pine for the regular appearance of friends for dinner, served in their fine china and pewter, and drinking the King's health afterward. While an occasional visitor still graced their table here, the sense of unifying defiance against the unruly elements of the community was missing, and the meals were scarcely better than cordial.

Re-reading in her primer the exhortation of John Rogers to his children, which he had supposedly composed just prior to his martyrdom, she was struck again by the unlikelihood of anyone condemned to death to have taken the time to get the rhyme and meter correct. The claim struck her as being of a piece with her father's assurance that their quiet life here would be more satisfying and restful than their interesting—albeit sometimes uncertain, as of late—existence back home.

> *Give ear my Children to my words,*
> *whom God hath dearly bought,*
> *Lay up his Laws within your heart,*
> *and print them in your thought,*
> *I leave you here a little Book,*
> *for you to look upon:*
> *That you may see your Father's face,*
> *when he is dead and gone.*

Without knowing quite why, Susannah found herself crying in spite of the questionable claim that these were the last words of a father to his children. If only she had some such statement of devotion from her mother, instead of just an old blanket and a wistful look in her father's eye when he mentioned how much she reminded him of her mother.

She set the book aside and wrapped herself in

the precious blanket until her tears subsided and sleep
claimed her.

Chapter 3

December the 29th

My dear friend Susannah,

I was filled with Joy at receiving your letter; it was a most unexpected pleasure to have had Communication from your outpost so soon after your sad Departure. I feel keenly your absence, and am fairly bursting with things to tell you about. Paper is dear in these troubled Days, however, so I will restrain myself to only a few anecdotes. I am happy to relate that my especial Friend Ezekiel has taken up a Position of some responsibility, helping to guard the King's custom house at the docks. He looks fine and tall standing watch, and he has bravely and patiently borne the Taunts of the rebellious rowdy boys who come around from time to time. Some of those selfsame rowdy boys or their Brothers in Spirit have committed a heinous Act, which I hesitate to relate, but which is so much on my mind in these days at the end of the year that I cannot but spare a few lines with which to unburthen myself to you. As you know, not far down the Coast from our formerly happy home is that precious Relic of the Arrival, the very Rock at which the Pilgrims alit at the end of their perilous Voyage hither. A crowd of Rowdy Boys determined to take it Prisoner to their own cause, and made to spirit it away to stand at their accursed so-called Liberty Tree. In the process of moving the Rock, they instead broke it into two

pieces, and being of little Fortitude, suffered Half of the rock to lie in state where it fell, bringing the other to their blasphemous Shrine. I cannot but think that this is a Sign that they will find some measure of success in their efforts, but will in the process Break our People into Two Parts, transporting one part to places distant and foreign to us. As I write this Line, I realise that this Cruel Fate has already befallen my dear friend and correspondent, and my Tears threaten to pollute this Page. I shall turn now for a few lines of happier news. Our friend Louise, whom you will recall had been courting with a fine Man from nearer the Frontier, has announced her Promise to be joined with him in the happy Institution of matrimony this spring next. My heart overflows for her everlasting Joy, and I hope only that she is not contaminated by his family's Whiggish Tendencies. No mean political difference can stand in the way of the heart's true Desire, though, and I know that you will join me in wishing her all possible Joy of her engagement and hope for her fulfillment without regard for these Troubled Days. Please write soon and pour out the Inmost secrets of your heart to me without fear. I am particularly Intrigued by the details of your new Tutor, about which you were most mysterious in your former letter. Until I shall again hold your words to my breast, I am, your friend,
  Emma

Susannah put the letter into its hiding place in her writing box and smiled. Dear Emma—so like her to be convinced that there must be something more to her relations with Master Grant than a mere tutelage. She smiled more broadly yet at the idea of him dreaming to make bold with her in any small way. Why, he would probably faint dead away at the mere thought.

Shaking her head and still smiling, she put the writing box away and pondered the rest of the letter. It certainly sounded as though things had gotten no better since her departure, and indeed, in some measures worse. The incident Emma had related of the rock at Plymouth sent a chill down her spine. It was, indeed, as though Providence itself was offering a warning to these colonies—set aside your petty differences or else suffer the fate hitherto visited only upon a lifeless rock.

The letter was silent on a question that had been foremost in Susannah's mind, but one that she dared not so much as give voice, so much did she fear to hear the answer. She had heard tales of other homes of departed Tories being ransacked and their contents put up to public auction. Were the rebellious mob so vindictive and sure of themselves in her town that they would dare to treat her home so?

She could not help but imagine her favorite chair, or the broad-boarded dinner table that had hosted any number of spirited discussions, or even the great cast iron pot she had spent so many dull hours with, all held up for the scrutiny of neighbors, friendly or otherwise, and then handed over for a pocket's worth of coins. The vision made tears spring to her eyes—so many things, it seemed, had that power in these grey and cold days—and she resented the frequency with which she succumbed to the urge toward such womanly expression.

The new neighbors in this place did not make it any easier. Beset with an influx of immigrants from over the seas, the townspeople did not trouble themselves to make the fine distinction between newly-arrived farmers, hungry for the fulfillment of a promise of free land and all that they might require upon which to build a proper homestead, and merely displaced fellow colonists, their own people in every regard but for the locale which they called home. She and her father made no demands upon the governor, but instead quietly arranged for a home and livelihood on their own.

And yet, the girls of her age would scarcely speak to her on the street, and when her back was turned, she could hear them affecting the broad Yorkshire accent, and giggling behind hands raised delicately to their mouths. It was all she could do to suffer these taunts in dignified silence; even if they could not tell the difference between a raw and uncouth immigrant and the daughter of a prosperous colonial merchant, the truth of her station lived in her heart.

Drying the tears at the corners of her eyes, Susannah resolved to put on a brave face and decline to give her tormentors the satisfaction of a reaction. Today, her father had told her, there would be goods in from Quebec, and she was to direct the delivery of his order to the house while he was away conducting some crucial business inland.

While she'd have preferred that the deliverymen could have simply been told where to bring the goods, he had insisted that she supervise the loading and carriage by sledge from the dry goods merchant to their house. She supposed that he had sufficient experience with the phenomenon of a load shrinking in transit by inexplicable means that he felt it necessary that she maintain a watchful eye throughout the process.

Peering out the window, she could see that it was a blustery day, though the fires that her father had laid in the kitchen and main room fireplaces were keeping the house quite cozy. She'd only had to add a few logs since his departure that morning, and before donning the greatcoat he'd had made for her from the skin of an enormous bear, she carefully placed another large piece of wood on each fire, to provide enough fuel that she would not need to re-start them upon her return.

As she shrugged on the new coat, she wrinkled her nose—almost more as reflex now, rather than in reaction to any remaining smell—remembering how the freshly-cured pelt had smelled when her father had brought it home from the tanner's. He insisted that it had been thoroughly cleaned; she was equally adamant that it still reeked of bear and the tanning process.

She felt bad for having been so ungracious, though, as it really was the warmest coat she had ever beheld. Even with the bitterest cold of their first winter in this place, she could spend better than an hour outside before winter's tenacious fingers began to reach through the garment and chill her. An old beaver hat, bought from a trader departing for warmer climes, and heavy boots completed her outdoor winter ensemble. Though she knew that none might look twice at her for the attractiveness of her appearance, she would remain warm for the entire time she was to spend out of doors today.

Winters at home could sometimes be hard, but here, it seemed much darker and gloomier than she was used to. She supposed that she could feel its grip loosening, and the long nights of the midwinter giving way slowly, ever so slowly, to earlier sunrises and later sunsets, but she yearned for the return of the long, warm days of summer.

Assuring herself that everything was in order, she closed the door behind herself and trudged down the frozen, snow-covered lane toward the mercantile in the grey light that passed for the midday sun under a sullen sky. As she walked, her mind wandered back to home, where this task would have been lightened by the company of Emma or another friend, and where the merchant and his draymen knew her father well enough—even if only by reputation—that it would have been unthinkable that supervision by Susannah or himself was needed. For what seemed like the hundredth time that day, she sighed heavily, turning the corner to the street where the mercantile stood, surrounded by sledges and activity.

Chapter 4

March the Fifth,
anno domini Seventeen Hundred & Seventy-Five

My dear friend Emma,
We are, I am assured, past the worst part of the winter in
this strange & uncomfortable place.   Though the snow yet piles
up without, & ice forms on the wrong side of the windows within,
those who have endured the turning of the seasons for many years
claim that the air is already sweeter, that the birds of a happier air
already arrive, & that they can detect the first shoots of Spring in
the buds of the trees. I cannot bear witness to these things, however,
as I am abed these past weeks with an injury of the ankle, arising
in an ill-considered step whilst doing the bidding of my beloved
father. The good people at the mercantile saw me fall & rushed to
my aid, but the damage was done, & I can yet make no step upon
that foot without there is more pain than ever I have experienced
in my life before. I do not lay any blame upon my Papa, although I
think that he may secretly harbour regret that I was out in the frozen
& uncertain streets to transact a business matter that he might
ordinarily have handled personally. No matter. Our neighbour, the
spinster Miss Vincent, is greatly learned in the proper treatment of
injuries such as mine. It is certain that she sees them in abundance
during the dismal season of the year, & she has both bound it &

prepared draughts for me to knit the hurts back together. She is a kindly soul, & I can tell that she means well, though the draughts make my stomach rebel almost as forcefully as the troublemakers back home, ha-ha. Speaking of those unwholesome fellows, what news have you of their latest fell exploits? Have they continued to molest the King's appointed representatives without provocation, or are they sensible to the consequences of continuing to resist the Parliament's firm but measured actions? I was most distressed to learn—by a news-paper brought home by my father—that instead of seeing that they could not hope to prevail against our King, that the representatives of the several colonies have pledged to join in response to any attack that they might provoke. Where I had hoped to learn that we might return to our natural home, I now despair at the thought of you suffering under a civil war, in our own formerly happy community. How can some men be so wicked as to pursue such ends, without any regard for the irreparable harm that they do by drawing violence against themselves & their neighbours? I apologize—I had to set this aside for a moment & regain my composure, as these bitter thoughts are simply too much to bear at times. What happy news have you of our friends? Has your interest in the admirable Mister Ezekiel Mills been noted & returned yet? How fares Louise & her declared love? As for myself, you may reassure yourself that I have no designs upon my tutor, Master Grant. He is a shy youth, & has no interest in any matter that he cannot find in the proceedings of the Royal Society, of which he is an avid reader. Indeed, I think that he may spend every coin he earns for his tutelage of me in the mundane subjects that I will suffer to learn on volumes of the Philosophical Transactions

of the same, which he orders by correspondence from London. He certainly does not spend any amount not utterly necessary on his clothing or on attending to his appearance, which is often shabby & frightful, respectively. Whatever musings you may have had about our Master Grant you may put entirely out of your mind. Until I shall read your welcome words again, I remain,
>   *Your affectionate friend,*
>   *Susannah*

Setting the writing board aside, Susannah shifted about uncomfortably in her bed, trying to find some position that reduced the dull throb of pain from her leg. The really alarming swelling that had initially accompanied her injury had now gone down, but she was alert to its return. Her foot had looked like a thing of nightmares, the skin stretched out as though it were a bladder filled with some sort of liquor.

There were still weird and frightening colors to behold on the shin, near where the injury seemed to have manifested, but even that was becoming less marked with every passing day. For this much, she was grateful, though reluctant to credit Miss Vincent's horrible draughts, for fear that such might encourage that indomitable lady. Susannah's father expressed great faith in her knowledge, and support for her suggestions, but there was something about the way that they looked at each other that made the girl uncomfortable.

No matter, in time all wounds are healed, and Susannah could already turn her foot about with far less pain than in the miserable days just after her accident. Though she hadn't wanted to write to Emma of it—knowing how eager that girl would be to find some romantic intrigue in it—the only good part of that horrid day had been when the shopkeeper's assistant had picked her up from the ground where she lay and carried her gently inside. In spite of her pain, she could not help but notice that he did not seem burdened in any significant way by the weight of her in his arms, and despite his stolid silence throughout her ordeal, she had noticed—and recollected frequently, with interest—the concern in his eyes for her comfort and well-being.

Surrounded by the crowd that had been drawn by her cries of pain, he had set her down carefully on a countertop the shopkeeper had hurriedly cleared. His wife, summoned from the kitchen, had quickly taken charge of the situation.

"You men clear out of here," she said crisply, and Susannah was only slightly surprised to see the crowd, even the shopkeeper, move to obey with alacrity.

Once they were alone in the shop, she said to Susannah, "I am sorry, my child, but I must take these boots off before that ankle swells up so big that we'd have to cut the thing off your foot."

In her confusion and pain, it took Susannah a moment to recognize that the woman was not warning of the possibility of amputation, but destruction of her footwear. The momentary confusion helped to distract her as the woman raised Susannah's skirt enough to undo her laces and slowly pulled the suddenly tight boot off her foot.

Susannah realized that she had passed out from the pain of the procedure when she looked up and saw the shopkeeper's wife looking fiercely at both of her unshod feet together, shaking her head and tut-tutting to herself.

"Well, child, you have certainly done greater harm

to yourself than is within my power to correct. We shall have to send you home and have Alma Vincent come around to physic you."

She looked up from Susannah's legs and a more kindly expression came over her face. "You'll be Richard Mills' daughter, won't you?"

Silently, Susannah nodded, not trusting her voice to keep from breaking in emotion. She had failed her father in the relatively simple task which he had asked her to complete, and had injured herself in the process. She could not yet know how badly she had hurt herself, but she did know that she had never in her life felt pain of this exquisite quality before.

The shopkeeper's wife nodded, saying, "I'm Patricia MacFarland, though I suppose your Pa will be wanting you to call me Missus MacFarland. We've got his order together, what we have of it, at least, and we'll just load you on the sledge with it, wrapped up snug and warm, all right?"

Again, Susannah just nodded.

The woman's face underwent another transformation, from the kindly, mothering expression to one of borderline annoyance as she flipped the hem of Susannah's skirt down to cover the girl's feet and then bellowed out, "All right, you laggards, back in here and get to work! We've an order to complete, and we need to get this girl on home."

She winked back at Susannah and smiled quickly. "Can't let them think that I'm all sweetness and light, now can I? They wouldn't get a single blessed thing done if I didn't stay on them. You just come on down here, and I'll get you into a chair whilst the boys load up your sledge."

Wrapping Susannah's arm around her solid

shoulder, the woman helped the girl down off the counter and half-carried her over to a chair up against the wall, helping her keep the hurt foot entirely off the ground. Susannah winced at the movement, but was glad to note that she did not feel faint again.

"Here, sit yourself down, and I'll go fetch you something to drink. It won't stop your ankle from hurting, but it might make the trip back to your house a bit easier to bear."

"Thank you, Missus MacFarland," Susannah said, unsteadily. The woman nodded curtly, her motherly persona completely masked again, and went back to her kitchen.

After a few minutes, during which she could hear the woman giving instructions to the men, the shopkeeper's wife returned holding a mug full of steaming liquid, which she pressed into Susannah's hands. "You drink that all down, do you understand? It might not be the most tasty thing you've ever had, but it will help you get through this next little bit of unpleasantness."

Susannah nodded and sniffed at the mug. Mostly, it just smelled like the rum that her father sometimes drank after supper, but the warmth of the steam drove fumes from the beverage into her nose, making her eyes water for a moment. She glanced up at the woman uncertainly, and was rewarded with a stern look. "Drink it anyway, if you know what's good for you. The boys will be done soon, and you'll be glad to have this in you when you get onto that sledge."

Susannah nodded and took a sip. The concoction wasn't as unpleasant as she'd feared it would be, and before long, it was finished, and the shopkeeper's wife gave her an approving glance as she took the empty mug from her.

"Let's get you loaded up, then. Here, take my arm. Got your boots already loaded in with the rest of your goods. That's it, good, up you go." As they started to walk together, though, Susannah cried out in pain at the movement, and the older woman had to relent.

Lowering the girl back into the seat, she said gruffly, "I'll have Colin come and carry you again, since the great ox already proved he could lift you easily enough."

In a small voice, Susannah replied, "Thank you, Missus MacFarland. I tried, but the pain was really more than I could take." The older woman grimaced and nodded, and went back outside to call to Colin.

When the young man followed her back inside, Susannah could have sworn that he was blushing as he bent to lift her a second time, but she stifled the thought as she focused on guiding her feet through the doorway such that they would not risk a painful collision.

In mere moments, he had her deposited—again, with remarkable gentleness—on the seat that the men had prepared for her among the goods on the sledge, and Missus MacFarland was busily arranging a thick woolen blanket carefully around her bare feet to keep them warm on the trip to her house.

By the time they arrived at the house, the drink had made Susannah light-headed enough that she scarcely took notice when Colin brought her inside and placed her on her bed. He nodded at her and seemed in a hurry to join the other men in noisily unloading the sledge into the house. Quickly enough, the job was done, and he returned to her door.

He asked, in a thickly-accented and quiet voice, "I've stoked the fires so that they'll be warming the house for you, and your Pa's order is all set in the kitchen. Is there anything else you'll be needing, Miss Mill, or will you be okay until Miss Vincent arrives to physic you?"

Susannah drew her blanket up to her chin, feeling suddenly chilled, and shook her head. "I—I think I'll be fine, Colin. Call me Susannah, won't you please?"

"Of course. Well, I'll see you up and around soon, I hope." He blushed again and dipped his head in farewell as he backed out of the room. She heard the front door close, and sank back onto her bed, willing the pain to subside.

Now, weeks later, she wished that she had been able to be out and about, if only to assist her father in his next trip to the mercantile. She folded the letter to Emma and sealed it, set it aside for her father to send with the next available post, and closed her eyes to get some rest.

Chapter 5

May the Ninth

My dear friend Susannah,

    I am certain that you have already heard the Shocking News from these parts, but I must relate the Details as I know them, for I am not utterly convinced that at your present remove, you can gain any clearer a View than your faithful friend may offer you from her own hand. The whole of the Region has been increasingly under the sway of the Evil sentiments of those who Desire to effect a break from their Sovereign, and out of a great concern for the Safety of his loyal subjects, he has sent great numbers of men under arms to these Shores. These several weeks ago, a mass of the King's Men were sent to investigate a Rumour of unrest. As they attempted to pass over the road at the town of Lexington, they were challenged by a well-armed Mob, and responding to that Challenge, they did fire upon the Rebellious Forces, striking some number of them down on the spot. Continuing their march, the victorious Forces of the Crown arrived then at the town of Concord, whereupon they were attacked by Cowards and Knaves who had taken up their positions out of clear sight, among the hills that lay about the Town. Out of an abundance of Prudence, the wise Commanders appointed by the King determined to return to their Quarters and seek reinforcement against the Menace of their Wicked Foes. All along the way, they were subjected to

Barbaric and Disorderly fire, directed upon them from many divers and widespread Hiding-Places. I have been told, and have no reason to doubt, that these Beasts pursued the Deliberate Design of laying low with preference the brave Officers leading the King's Men. It shatters my heart to relate to you that by the end of this Engagement of Arms, over one Hundred brave and loyal Subjects in Uniform lay in unsought blood, marking a most terrible day in the Annals of History. Tho through the Grace of Providence, he was not present at this confrontation, I am filled with Fear for my Precious Friend Ezekiel. I pray daily for our Deliverance from this Time of Trouble and Woe, but the countryside all about is now Aroused in rage, and I fear that it will only be a matter of Time before this Spark shall ignite all the tinder that has been Stored in the hearts of men of good Conscience and ill. These are fearful days, and I shudder to realise that they are Fated to pass during our time. I add to my Prayers the most fervent wishes for your Speedy Recovery from your hurts, and the hope that these Disorders shall not reach the shores to which your father has relocated you with such Foresight. I have broken entirely with Louise, as she has fallen under the fell Influence of her bridegroom's Sympathies with the Troublemakers who seek to undermine the King. We had quite an animated Argument over the terrible Events which I have here related to you, and we resolved on the spot to have no more to do with each other. Begging the Benign Ruler of the Universe for your safety and comfort, I am,

> *Your Devoted Friend,*
> *Emma*

Susannah set the letter down with a shaking hand,

and said to her father, "Papa, I had heard of the recent violence near our former home, but I did not previously appreciate how very grave the incident was."

He looked up from where he sat working his accounts and sighed, "Yes, my dear child, it was very nearly a spark in a tinderbox, but it is to be hoped that less unquiet voices will prevail upon the more excitable souls among them, and cause them all to consider the consequences, should they not step back from the brink of a break with the mother country."

Susannah frowned. "Perhaps you should read the letter that Emma sent to me, Papa. If anything, her words persuade me that the fuse to the powderkeg is now lit, and we may expect to feel the explosion even at this remove."

She handed the page over to him, and he accepted it, reading Emma's fine penmanship without difficulty. Susannah's mouth quirked at the thought that Emma likely still suffered under Miss Thayer's constant remonstrations to more carefully form her letters, while Master Grant cared only for whether he could make sense of what was written. As a result, Susannah, thought, her pen was probably less fine than once it had been, while Emma's would continue to profit by Miss Thayer's attentions, so long as events permitted such normal things as lessons and correspondence to continue.

Frowning deeply, her father folded the letter and handed it back. "I agree that it sounds as though we have not heard the whole of the story here, but I will also note that your friend Emma is an excitable sort of girl, and so we must no more than take under advisement any opinion of the mood of the countryside that she might advance."

Susannah considered this for a moment, and then replied, "Nonetheless, I am now grateful that you took the precaution of removing us to this place. Perhaps I have been filled with resentment for having to abandon the comfort of our home, but I now realize that it was a false comfort, concealing great hazards to our safety."

Her father regarded her seriously. "I knew that it would be a shock, and a great hardship upon you to depart from all that you had known and held dear, but I knew also that to stay would be to run the risk of exposing you to the hazards of war."

His brow gathered tightly and his eyes closed as he shook his head sadly. "I did not dream that it would come so openly or soon, however. I fear now for the security of our friends who remain, and indeed, I tremble for the future of our happy experiment on these shores. Can any nation hope to maintain harmony with a far-flung empire of colonies, if the British Sovereign and our advanced system of law cannot? Can any nation hope even to persist as a nation for a span of years greater than the reign of a particularly enlightened king?"

With a sour look, he waved a dismissive hand. "Please forgive me for ranting so. I forget at times that I am not at my table of peers, and that your interests are far different from the high questions of philosophy that haunt the depths of our cups."

"No, Papa, you forget that I have oft overheard you and your friends in your debates and discussions, and find them reliably informative and intriguing. Our old house, for all its many charms, did not conceal the sound of voices raised in banter from one room to the next, and even as I was supposed to be sleeping, it was common enough for me to be marking your words."

She blushed slightly and added, "Even though I

knew that you might again chastise me, I did sometimes open the door, that I might hear more clearly when a discussion was of special interest. I know that it was beyond the boundaries of propriety to listen to your private conversations, but in truth there was much that I could not help but hear, were I even tight in my bed."

He nodded, his expression still sour, conceding the point. "I feared that I was keeping you awake during our midnight tables, but as you never complained, I thought that you were a sound sleeper enough to withstand our voices." Giving her a wry smile, he said, "Perhaps it is for the best; thus are you better informed than would otherwise be the case."

"In any event, Papa, you have not yet found the joy of such society in this place, and while I would not now trade our security here for that pleasure there, I do not fancy myself to be an equal to the conversational skills of your friends."

He gave her a quick smile and said, "Your quest for compliments is noted and rewarded—I do not lack for interesting discussions in your company. As for the society of my friends, why, we may yet see them here, should events in our former home not improve."

They were interrupted by a rapping at the door, and he sprang to his feet. "That will be Miss Vincent, here to examine the progress of your ankle's repair. When I saw her yesterday, I asked her to pay us the compliment of her company at dinner tonight."

Susannah could hear him giving final instructions to the cook, a girl of her own age named Michelle, whose Yorkshire parents were improving a farmstead in a valley not a day's ride distant, but whom they placed with her father so as to earn some hard money to support their enterprise. She was, for the most part, exceptionally competent in the kitchen—indeed, Susannah privately thought that she must study under the girl once her ankle was well enough—and severely quiet, speaking only in response to direct queries.

After the front door closed, she could hear Miss Vincent's gentle voice as her father took her cloak for her. After a moment, they reappeared in the informal sitting room, and Susannah gingerly rose to her feet to greet her.

"It is so good to see you up on your feet," exclaimed the healer, stepping forward to take Susannah's hands in her own. "Your color is much improved today, as well. Please, do sit, and allow me to examine your feet before we must go to the kitchen for dinner."

Susannah sat, saying, "I appreciate your kindness, Miss Vincent. I think I shall soon be ready to walk about on my own again, though perhaps with the aid of crutches of some description." Behind Miss Vincent, her father smiled at her determination.

Miss Vincent knelt on one knee before Susannah's chair and took the injured foot up onto her own raised leg. She rapidly unbound it, her fingers working with such gentleness that Susannah did not so much as flinch even once. She motioned for the girl to raise her other foot to sit beside the hurt one, and stared at them both, then grasped the toe of each and began gently moving them in unison, first in one direction and then in another. At a couple of points of motion, Susannah grimaced, and once she gasped aloud as a particularly sharp pain resulted from the movement.

Taking her hands off Susannah's feet, Miss Vincent rubbed them together and nodded, smiling. "I think that is probably a good next step, yes. We can talk to someone in town who has some skill with tools, and have a pair manufactured for you, if your father agrees."

He nodded, saying with a smile, "If I do not agree, she will likely attempt to go for a stroll even without the support of proper crutches, and then undo all of your fine work."

Miss Vincent smiled back at him and took up the wrapping again to bind Susannah's ankle up again. As she worked, she asked, "Should you prefer your draught before we sup, or afterward?"

Susannah reflexively wrinkled her nose in distaste and said, "After, please, if it is no great inconvenience."

Miss Vincent laughed and replied, "None whatever. There, you are set to go. Shall we to the kitchen, Richard?"

Her father smiled, and something like a sparkle of joy shone in his eye as he replied, "Yes, Alma, just let me help Susannah to the table. You go on ahead."

Smiling again, Miss Vincent stood and moved aside so that Susannah could take her father's shoulder and follow them into the kitchen. Michelle had set the table with what finery they had fetched with them in their hasty departure, and a pewter tureen of fragrant soup stood steaming in the center.

As there was no place else for her to dine, she joined the family and their guest, although she stayed entirely silent throughout the meal, only blushing in response to the well-deserved praise that the diners offered her for her cooking.

Soup gave way to mutton, which was then followed by a savory pudding and a small glass of sack for each. The food and drink were accompanied by happy chatter, the somber mood brought on by Emma's letter now lifted with Miss Vincent's appearance.

More than once through the meal, Susannah thought that she caught her father and the healer looking at each other with something more than just casual friendship, but she dismissed the possibility—for as long as she could remember, it had been just her father and her, and she could not anticipate that even so gentle a soul as Miss Vincent might change that.

Soon enough, the final course had been cleared, and, after the noxious and unwelcome draught had been given, her father gathered Miss Vincent's cloak and helped her into it. Father and daughter stood together at the door to wave farewell to their friend, and after they closed the door, he said to her, "I will see to the crutches this evening, if you will promise me that you will not attempt to go abroad before they are delivered."

She gave him a wry smile and said, "Of course, Papa. I have no desire to give Miss Vincent cause to continue preparing those draughts for me—they really are dreadful."

He laughed and nodded. "'Tis a pact, then, and I shall maintain my end of it. I'll set off straightaway, if you will be comfortable enough with your reading?"

"If you will but help me back to my chair, I should be fine until your return. Michelle can attend to anything that I might need in your absence." The serving-girl nodded silent assent, and Susannah smiled at her father as he led her back to her chair.

Chapter 6

July the 7th, anno domini 1775

My Dear Friend Emma,
    We all pray for the safe deliverance of our distant friends from the convulsions of disorder & chaos that now grip our world. We read with dismay of the destruction visited upon those whom the King has sent to protect his loyal subjects, & we have received other reports of the terrible events of that day, as well. No such disruption seems imminent here. Indeed, the most substantial events are the jailing of a customs-house man & judge who, it is said, was embezzling from the amounts entrusted to him for benefit of the Crown, & a youth who died in a most bizarre incident involving a moose-deer the which he was apparently harassing. He was not anyone I knew, being named one Duncan Ellis, a recent arrival to these shores, & by all reports, not given to listening much to the advice of his peers or elders. My friend Colin told me the details of the incident, when he brought me a pair of crutches. My Papa procured them in order that I might regain the ability to move about the town again without I should need the assistance of a servant, & Colin was kind enough to bring them along in person. We fell into conversation when he delivered the blessed things, which he had manufactured by his own hands, taking pains to

ensure that they were well-fitted to my comfort & utility. He is a most entertaining young man, & his strength is enough that he could lift me bodily up from the mud where I fell this last winter. I passed several pleasant hours in discourse with him, & from him I have learned much of our situation here in Nova Scotia. There are many Scotsmen, naturally, & I may have mentioned the regular flood of Yorkshiremen who have lately been shipped over the seas hither, for the improvement of land abandoned by the Acadians who resided in these parts prior to its acquisition by the British Crown some few years past. The Yorkshiremen have been most energetic, though some have come bearing unreasonable expectations & demands. These demands having been disposed of, however, they are, for the most part, settling down & applying themselves with some energy to the land provided to them, & we soon shall want for very little, if Colin is correct. I am most gratified to read by your hand that your dear friend Ezekiel has weathered these dark days unscathed, & will continue to pray for your preservation & his safety. It grieves me to hear that our former friend Louise has taken up the wild ideas of the Rebels, & I think you are right to have broken with her. I cannot help but hope, though, that the breach may be repaired once this radicalism & foolishness has been settled by the King & by calmer heads. It may yet be some time before we see this come to pass, but I remain confident that the Ruler of All will not suffer to watch his favoured people torn asunder. We are bound to our mother country by ties which run deeper even than those of blood, & it will take more even than some blood

spilled to sever them. This is the subject of my most fervent prayers, alongside the safety & joy of my devoted friend. To this prayer, then, and I am,
>> *Your sincere friend,*
>> *Susannah*

Though she had but touched upon the turmoil that Colin's visit had caused her, Susannah still felt as though committing any part of the events of that afternoon to paper was to risk making it somehow evaporate like a morning mist in the sun. The moment of his arrival at the door had been as unexpected as it was heartening, and she remembered it fondly and frequently in the days since.

The rapping at the door was measured and firm, and she could hear Michelle open the door and greet their visitor. The girl showed him into the sitting room, and Susannah could feel a flush steal over her face as she beheld Colin, two unfinished crutches in his hands. He smiled and walked over to offer his hand, grasping hers in it when she responded in kind.

"'Tis good to see you again, Susannah, and you look to be in better sorts than when first we met."

She suppressed the flustered feeling that had come over her at beholding him and replied, "I am glad to see you, and happy to confirm that I am in far better condition than on our last meeting. I did not expect that you would be the person to bring over the crutches my Papa asked be made for me."

He grinned unabashedly, saying, "I had anticipated that you might need these after your accident, so since then I have been looking out for likely-looking pieces as I wandered the woods. I've left them unfinished, that we might measure and fit them particularly to you. Should you like to stand, that I may measure them against your height?"

She was taken aback by his thoughtfulness, and it was all she could do to nod in grateful acceptance. He leaned the unfinished crutches against the wall and took her hands in his to assist her in standing up from the chair. She could not help but notice that they were, though calloused and rough, gentle as he helped her.

"Right, then, just balance against me, and let us see how much I need to trim from the bottom of this one." He held the first crutch up beside her, adding, "Stand straight for a moment, if you would?" She wobbled slightly, but kept her balance as he closely examined where the top of the crutch fell against the side of her arm.

He blushed slightly as she looked over and smiled at the sight of him frowning at the padded handle of the crutch, marking with his eye how much he would need to trim. He carried the crutch over to the hearth and produced a small hatchet from within his jacket. With a single, sure stroke, he removed a finger-length from the bottom of the crutch and then handed it to her.

"Try that, and tell me if it feels comfortable, or if I should remove a bit more." She took it from his hand and tucked it under her arm, where it fit as though it had grown there. He laid the other crutch on the hearth and held out his hand for the first, that he might put them together and match their lengths. In a moment, he stood and presented them both to her.

"You should use them both at first, and Miss Vincent gave me strict instructions that you were to keep your injured foot off the ground until she should tell you otherwise. Once she has determined that your ankle will hold some weight, though, you can walk with but one, putting it under your arm on the unhurt side. That way, it will take some of the strain off your ankle."

She nodded and said, "She told me the same, and I am grateful that she bade you to remind me of her instructions."

He nodded encouragingly. "Let me see you try them?"

She took a step on her good foot and as she leaned forward, the two crutches swung ahead to take her weight as though she had always been using them. Her face lit up with a great smile, and she said, "These are perfectly marvelous—I cannot possibly repay you adequately for the care that you have taken on my behalf."

He grinned in response and said, "It was the least I could do after seeing you so cruelly laid low by your accident."

She dipped her face in embarrassment at the memory, and then motioned with her head toward the kitchen. "Would you join me for a bite to eat? Michelle was just about to lay out our meal when you arrived."

He looked startled for a moment at her offer, and said, carefully, "Will your father not disapprove of you taking a meal in the company of a guest while he is absent from your house?"

She shook her head, smiling. "My Papa knows that I have naught to fear from our neighbors here, and Michelle's presence with us will provide further assurance of the nature of our visit, if that be your concern."

He gave her a rueful look and said, "Indeed, it had crossed my mind that he might question my intentions in staying beyond the requirements of my service to him—and to you."

"Worry not," she said, and led the way into the kitchen. Over her shoulder, she said, "He will be glad to see me making some friend here, as my interactions with the people of this town have been no more than superficial—and I mean to correct that, beginning now."

Chapter 7

Twenty-First June, '75

My dearest Susannah

I write to you with a heart utterly Destroyed by the late Events in this Ruined Paradise. The worst News I shall dispense with first—our Friend Ezekiel has been Killed in the course of a brave Action, about which I shall say more when I have gathered my Ability to relate any words at all. You have, I am certain, long been acquainted with the Vicious Events that took place during the Summer past on the Heights overseeing that most admirable of Cities, our fair Boston-Town. The entirety of Charles-Town, which lay close by the hot Action of the summer, has been extinguished by fire promoted by the Evil actions of the rebels who infest the Countryside all about there. A pitched Battle was there fought, with the loss of some hundreds of gallant Souls, among the which was my dear Ezekiel. Oh! I cannot write anything Sensible, so lost am I in my Grief, but I shall try. The wicked Enemy (for Enemies they now be, to all decent Men of loyal hearts) made bold to attempt a Bombardment of the city of Boston, which was held firm under the Protection of the King's Men who have long been encamped in that Place. Our Men gave them firm opposition in this Cruel Design, and the battle that resulted was as Terrible as any I have read about in any History. While I was not present, that Place being, as

you know, pretty distant from our little Town, I have spoken to those who went there and Assisted to bury those who fell to our enemies' treacherous Designs. One of the fallen was found to have in his Pocket a letter signed as Ezekiel Mills, and when I described that Dear Man to he who carried the precious Letter, he agreed that the cold corpse answered to Ezekiel's description. I am unable to imagine my Fate without my friend and Protector, dear Susannah! I am overcome with the loss we have thereby suffered. In the end, as I am sure you have read in your news-papers, the Loyal forces of the King repulsed the cowardly attack of the accursed rebels, but such Victories we cannot afford very often, it is said far and wide. I cannot breathe, I am so consumed with grief, even with Ezekiel these many weeks in his cold Grave. There is not much else to tell that you will not have heard of elsewhere. We labour in the Desolation that is our world after this terrible Battle, and hope only that our Enemies may come to swift and complete Defeat and Ruin, as they have brought so many good Men to ruin. I hope that you are well, and that the Evil of war may not come to visit you at your Wise Remove from this place of Woe. I am,
    Your sad but constant Friend,
    Emma

Susannah felt her heart constrict in her chest, and she sat sobbing for her friend's losses, and for the unimaginable violence that now stalked the familiar places she had once known so well. The accounts of the battle on the approaches to Boston that had reached them so far had consisted mainly of dry recitations of the numbers of dead, wounded and captured on both sides, from which it seemed a wonder that the rebels should not have prevailed.

Hearing her distress, her father returned to her room, where she had, as was her habit, taken the letter when he had brought it home after being delivered it by the post. Without saying anything through her tears, Susannah handed him the letter, which was more difficult than most of Emma's to read, being spotted with what had to have been her tears.

She watched him reading it, and saw him turn white and clutch his hand to his mouth as he read. He sat heavily on the foot of her bed as he finished reading it, and when he was finished, he set it down and closed his eyes in a long moment of evident pain.

He sat, with his head bowed for a long while, and Susannah was incredulous at the sight of tears trickling from beneath his screwed-closed eyelids.

Susannah spoke, tentatively, "Papa?"

He took a deep breath and re-opened his reddened eyes, looking as though he had aged a decade since he had entered the room. "Susannah," he began, and his voice broke with emotion.

He shook his head angrily and started again, "Susannah, there is news in this letter that I had not looked to ever read, and it concerns matters that I had not looked to ever have to tell you about." He took another deep, shuddering breath.

"Papa, what—"

He held up his hand to silence her, and continued. "Please, just let me tell my tale without interruption. When I have finished, you may ask me questions, or send me from your room, if that be your will. But do let me finish first, I beseech you."

Unsure what this might be leading up to, Susannah nodded mutely, an unshaped fear growing in her gut as she waited for him to speak.

"Susannah, there are some things about our history which I have not so much kept hidden from you as I have neglected to tell you about. After I lost your mother, I was bereft in a manner that I hope from the core of my heart that you never have cause to feel. I could not imagine so much as rising from my bed in the morning, much less attending to the many needs of raising a newborn infant."

He paused to dab at his eyes and Susannah nodded slowly, understanding at least the boundaries of his loss, if not the depths. "Our neighbor's daughter Helen was dispatched to come to my aid, and she was like a mother to you, when you had none. In time, she helped to make my hurts better, as well, and soon enough, she had my heart."

He stopped with his eyes again closed and chewed his lips for a moment, as though to stop the next words from having to issue forth, but mastered himself and picked up his story. "Although some in the town thought it scandalous, being mere months after I lost your mother, it was inevitable that I should wed her, and in due time, she was got with child. All through her pregnancy, I was beside myself with fear, but she seemed to only grow healthier as our baby grew within her womb."

The tears poured from his eyes anew as he said, "I was right to fear, though, as my nightmare repeated itself, and I lost my second wife in childbirth. I resolved at that instant to never risk love or even attachment again, and I sent the child to live with Helen's relations as I buried her and learned how to raise you alone."

He stopped for a long, long moment, and then looked Susannah in the eye and concluded, "That child was your half-brother Ezekiel."

Chapter 8

August the 4th, a.d. Seventeen Seventy Five
My Precious Friend Emma,
    We are insensate with grief with our unlooked-for loss. After receipt of your letter, my father acquainted me with certain heretofore concealed facts. Ezekiel shared not only my surname—a fact upon which you & I have at divers times commented—but we also shared blood, as he was my half-brother by a stepmother whose sweet attentions were snatched from me by death's cruel hand before even my earliest memory. I am haunted, & even in my grief, charmed, by the thought that you & I might someday have become sisters, had your pursuit of my unsuspected half-brother borne less bitter fruit. If you do not object, I should like to think of you as my sister, drawn closer by our shared loss. My father is like a ghost in these terrible days, so great are his guilt & regret for what might have been. While Ezekiel suffered not for never having known who his blood father was—he was well provided-for in both kin & material means—Papa is wracked with the thoughts of what he ought to have done, rather than giving up a child for whom he was unequipped in every way to care in the wake of his second wife's death. There is no remarkable news here outside of this, so I close, sadly,
    Your Sister in Grief,

Susannah

Susannah folded and sealed the letter, and tucked it inside her gown for later delivery to the mercantile, where she could arrange to have it sent by the next post. She took a deep breath, willing the tears to dry from her eyes. Miss Vincent was due to come by soon, and there was no need for the healer to see her red-eyed and gasping yet again. Allowing herself some time to recover herself so as to be ready for company seemed a prudent idea.

When Susannah emerged from her room, now only using the crutches because Miss Vincent insisted, Michelle was quietly working at the kitchen table, cutting a handful of early apples for a tart she had proposed making that morning. Susannah raised a questioning eyebrow at her and indicated her father's door with a tilt of her head. Michelle shook her head silently. No appearance from him yet today.

Susannah settled herself in the comfortable chair in the sitting room and picked up her primer, leafing through it, more out of habit than any remaining necessity, as she had nearly the entire book committed to memory now. A page from the illustrated alphabet fell open, and she stifled a sob.

> *Xerxes the great did die*
> *And so must you and I*
> *Youth forward slips*
> *Death soonest nips*

Despite herself, the words brought her to recollect the time that she had spent, unaware of his relation to her, with Ezekiel. A serious youth, he had always been unfailingly polite to both her and Emma, though he had favored Emma from their earliest acquaintance. She wondered if he knew of their shared blood, and that was why he had never shown her any particular interest outside of casual friendship and childhood playmates. Although she knew that even then, the conflict that would end his life and alter her own had been building, the memories seemed golden and innocent. The happy distance between youthful play and the events of the larger world was scarcely violated, and she cherished the recollections of her half-brother with a new intensity.

Her reverie was brought to a sharp end by her father's door creaking open, and the emergence of his gaunt figure from the room. Forgetting her crutches, Susannah leapt to her feet and rushed over to embrace him.

Her head cradled against his shoulder as he patted her back, she asked quietly, "How do you fare today, Papa?"

"I shall survive this day, as I have others before it. It is time that I let the dead rest and get on with the business of living."

She hugged her father tighter at hearing the resolve in his words, even if his voice was still thin and drab.

While she continued to bask in his embrace, a knock sounded at the door, and Michelle went to go greet Miss Vincent and welcome her in. She entered the sitting room, and though she grimaced at Susannah upon seeing her up and about without the crutches, she said nothing, waiting quietly while father and daughter slowly released each other and shared a gentle smile full of forgiveness, hope, and resolve.

Susannah turned to the healer and took her hands. "It is so good to see you again, Miss Vincent. As you can see, I am well on the way to healing now."

"I do see that, yes. Please do sit now, though, so that I may examine your ankle." Miss Vincent smiled at the girl, shaking her head.

As Susannah returned to her chair, the healer turned to her father and grasped his hands warmly. "I am very glad to see you up and around again, Richard," she said, making no effort to conceal the depths of her relief and concern for his well-being.

He looked away for a moment, and then turned back to face her. "I cannot let the sadness of this world break me, Alma. The loss and pain that we experience between the cradle and the grave is all part of the plan of the great Author of the world to instruct our souls on the meaning of strength and faith."

He closed his eyes and released one of her hands to mop his brow before adding quietly, "I have not been so good a student, these past days, but I have determined to accept this lesson with as much grace as I can muster."

Finally, he pulled Miss Vincent into a long embrace, to which her initial response was awkward and stiff. After Susannah gave her a quick smile and then looked away, saying without words that she would suspend any feelings of shock or embarrassment this sight might ordinarily have caused her, the healer relaxed into his arms, and stood there for a long moment, a small smile on her lips.

Finally, Susannah's father released her, and she gave him a final pat on the back before stepping away and turning to Susannah. As usual, she knelt on one knee before the girl, and lifted the injured foot to sit on her upright leg. As he took his seat in the other chair in the room, Miss Vincent said, "Let us take a look at this healed joint, then, shall we?"

Her fingers, as always gentle and strong, pulled the house slipper from Susannah's foot, and unbound the ankle. Susannah wrinkled her nose at the smell of the closely-wrapped flesh as it was revealed to the open air and gave Miss Vincent an apologetic look.

"Do not worry, my dear. I am inured to such things, and believe me when I say that this is far from the worst I have ever beheld." Susannah looked away, abashed, and Miss Vincent smiled at her. Running through the familiar motions of pulling and then pushing on Susannah's toes, and waiting for the girl to push and then pull in response, she watched the ankle intently as it moved through the range of actions she was asking of it.

Probing with her fingertips along the joint, she asked, "Does this give you any pain?"

"No, Miss Vincent, no pain at all. I do believe that I could dispense with the wrappings and crutches now."

The woman gave her a look of mock sternness. "Dear child, do you want to spend yet more months bedridden and in agony? The bones may be knit, but they still bear the marks of their rupture, and may be broken again with less effort than on your first attempt to hobble yourself for life. Heed my instructions, or you may well find success on your next attempt."

Susannah giggled at Miss Vincent's fierce expression, and the older woman's glare dissolved into a smile of her own. "In all seriousness, Susannah, you must continue to wrap it for some weeks after you last feel any twinge of pain, and continue to relieve the pressure of its use by relying upon the crutches for longer yet."

Her father spoke up, saying, "You would do well to heed Miss Vincent's wise counsel, Susannah. 'Tis born of much learning and no small amount of observation and experience."

The girl frowned, but nodded her head. "I shall hew as closely to your advice as ever I can, Miss Vincent."

Michelle entered the room from the kitchen and said quietly, "Dinner is ready, if you should like to eat now."

Susannah's father smiled and said, "I could eat until the sun set, I am so famished. Let us repair to the kitchen and set to without any delay."

Miss Vincent stood and helped Susannah to her feet, handing her the accursed crutches with a firm little smile. For her part, Susannah refrained from rolling her eyes until the healer had looked away, and they were all on their way into the kitchen.

The next day, crutches firmly under her arms, Susannah set out for the mercantile. The town, which had seemed so strange and foreign when they had first arrived, now felt safe and familiar. Though few of her neighbors had warmed to her completely, she was at least able to greet many of them by name now, and the sight of her hobbling through the streets excited little comment, either within her earshot or after she had passed.

Entering the shop, she was pleased to see that Missus MacFarland was holding court behind the till. The shopkeeper's wife caught her eye as she entered.

"So good to see you up and around, Susannah," she called, and then turned to the small ground of men with whom she'd been holding an intense discussion. "Mark my words, there'll be no such disorders in this place. There may be a criminal element the representatives of which might believe that they may be able to commit mayhem unchecked, but we will take what steps we must to combat that tendency."

One of the men shook his head and replied, "I hear of plenty enough who seek to stir up the sentiments of the countryside against the King. The rebels' agents are active and energetic in sowing discord far beyond its seat in that rotten town of Boston, the which was never satisfied with any concession that might be made to it, and whose inhabitants and all the surround are but criminals and rabble."

Her expression fixed, Susannah advanced and stepped up to the till. She extracted the sealed letter to Emma from her gown and said, with deliberate clarity, "Missus MacFarland, might you be so kind as to hold this letter for the next ship to Boston"—she stressed the words with a sudden fierceness—"nearby where my correspondent resides, that it may be introduced to the post for delivery thence?"

Giving the outspoken man a firm look, Missus MacFarland took the letter from Susannah's hand and placed it beneath the counter. "Surely, my dear. How fares your ankle?"

Susannah smiled at her, and ignored the men around the till completely. "I am assured that, though it is healing marvelously and gives me no more pain at all, I am not to trust it any more than I would a brittle piece of kindling, lest I shatter it anew."

"Best follow that advice, though I can see that it chafes. Do you need anything more brought around? We are short on most everything, the trade being so disrupted, but your father is a good and loyal customer, so if there is anything you lack, just say the word." She seemed to be putting extra stress on her words, as well, and Susannah smiled in appreciation.

"I believe that we are well provisioned at this time, Missus MacFarland, but I do appreciate the offer, and will convey it to Papa. I had best be on my way, before I corrupt any of these fine men with my criminal roots." She smiled sweetly at the loudmouthed man, and he gawped at her in response.

As she turned to leave, he called after her, "I meant no disrespect, Miss. I was only repeating what I have heard elsewhere, and I will make every effort to be more fair minded."

She turned back and said, "You may believe as you wish, but know this: no people anywhere are an undivided mass. Every community has its shame, and every community its pride. Good people may be found wherever one bothers to look."

Without pausing to hear what he might say in reply, she turned back to the door and made her way out into the sunshine. As she exited, her heart hammering in her chest over the confrontation, she felt a moment of dismay at finding Colin approaching the mercantile. She gathered herself quickly, though, and mustered a smile for him.

"A good day to you, Miss Susannah," he said formally, motioning as though to sweep his nonexistent hat from his tousled head.

She smiled at him in spite of herself, and replied, "And a fine day to you, too, Master Colin. I don't suppose that you are at liberty to escort me to my home?"

He pondered for a moment, and then said, "I do not see any reason that I cannot do so. Shall we?" He reflexively offered his arm, and then checked himself, glancing ruefully at the crutches. "I shall be most pleased to see you quit of those things," he said.

"I quite like them," she replied. "I am reluctant to give them up, knowing that you fashioned them with your own hands with so much care." She gave him a bold smile and fell in beside him.

As they walked, she said quietly, "Papa is out of his room today, and I think he will return to himself fully now."

He looked at her sharply. "I am glad for that," he said. "Has he said anything further about your half-brother?"

"Not anything properly about Ezekiel, no, although he has had much to say to his walls about the cruelty of fickle fate, and the foolishness of mortal choices."

"I cannot find anything to dispute with him on either point," Colin said, his brow beetling. "Both are true, and yet both we can but stand against."

"He said much the same this afternoon," Susannah replied. They walked along in silence for a while, and then she said, "Have you any brothers or sisters? I am abashed that I have not inquired previously."

He shrugged and said, "I have one brother, who has taken up on a farm with a Yorkshire family. I have not spoken with him in better than a year, and it may be better than a year before we speak again, and I do not expect that either of us will miss the other very much."

Susannah let the comment lie for another few steps and then said, "I am sorry to hear that, my friend. I should think that anyone who knew you would miss your company." She blushed, but continued, "I know that I enjoy our conversations, and should feel the loss if we were unable to continue them for some reason."

He smiled at her and said, "Then you are either more tolerant or wiser than my brother." They turned the corner to the road where her house stood, and he said, "However, our conversation today seems to have been abbreviated by your ever-speedier pace. I almost miss the times when you could scarcely hobble at all, and we had half the afternoon to converse."

She laughed aloud, and realized that it was the first time she had laughed since the letter bearing the fatal news had arrived. She felt a flash of gratitude toward Colin, and was all the more reluctant to say her farewell as she opened the door to enter her house. She stood in the entrance for a moment, waving, and then reluctantly closed the door behind her.

Within, Michelle was finishing with the evening's washing, and her father was again nowhere in evidence. When she gave Michelle a questioning look again, the girl blushed deeply and whispered, "He has retired to his room. With Miss Vincent."

Chapter 9

Seventeenth September, anno domini 1775

My Dear Sister Emma,

    I write with no assurance that you have received my prior letter, due to later terrible events which have befallen our community. Less terrible, to be sure, than what you have there experienced, but shocking to our felicity. To rehearse what we said in my last letter to you, which may be providing entertainment to some rebellious mind instead of comfort to my dear friend, your particular friend Ezekiel was, unknown to me, also my half-brother Ezekiel, so our loss & pain are shared in greater measure than ever we expected. Mere days after I dispatched my last letter—days which were in their own ways, eventful, tho now overshadowed in the extreme— we here beheld the strange & outrageous sight of a privateer, or more precisely, a brigand pirate, sailing into our harbour with intentions of visiting ruin upon all that his guns & vile crew could reach. By the blessings of the Almighty, he spared the town, but he sailed around to the fort at the river Saint John, which guards the Western approaches to our district, & burnt it to the ground, as well as along the way seized several ships engaged in the trade between here & Boston, & points South & East. Indeed, it is for this reason that I believe it possible that my last letter to you may have been waylaid in the course of its passage to you. The posts are,

I know, a chancy thing at all times during a war, but it distresses me more than I can say to feel the press of warfare so close by my shores. I anticipate that you may appreciate this sentiment, & may even find it overwrought in light of the relatively minor threat under which we are watchfully waiting. Between our loss & the constant fear that some marauding band of rebels will sneak past the militia that drills constantly in our streets, & perform some act of barbarism, & the constant stream of notices of the same in the country around, it is difficult to think of any matter of normal concerns. I must spare a few lines, however, on the scandalous conduct of my own Papa with the spinster healing-woman to whose care he had committed me in my late injury. He has taken up with her in a most public & unashamed manner, & I cannot help but think that the general lawlessness of this age has corrupted the regulation of his heart's urges. Miss Vincent is a very decent sort, & I cannot find it in my heart to hold her to blame for the affair in which she & Papa are embroiled. At the moment, they have kept their liaison within the walls of our home & hers, but even with the worries of an ongoing threat of mob violence upon their persons & community, it can only be so long before our neighbours may notice. Here, as everywhere, the villagers are watchful. Alas, all of these matters stand in the way of my pursuit of even the most wholesome of interests in my friend Colin. I fear that he must feel quite bewildered at my failure to respond in any overt way to his many kindnesses & well-placed attentions. I cannot find room in my heart to ponder these possibilities, though, with so much else crowding them out at present. I pray that this letter reaches you, despite the cordon of ruffians it must penetrate before it reaches the watchful supervision of the ships we are told are now picketed in

our defence. I hope to hear from you soon, & until then, I am,
    Your Sister in Grief & Worry,
    Susannah

With a deep sigh, Susannah folded and sealed the letter, and then stood—the crutches can go to the devil, she caught herself thinking with uncharacteristic venom—and called out, "Michelle, I shall return shortly, as I have a letter to dispatch to the post."

The girl emerged from the kitchen and replied, "Very good, Miss Susannah. Did Mister Mills inform you of his plans for the afternoon, or shall I prepare the table for just the two of us?"

"No, he did not, and if he is not returned by the time I have done with my business, well, then, he can eat a cold crust by the hearth, for all of me." Susannah did not like hearing the coldness in her tone, nor did the frustration in her heart set well with her.

She was becoming a bitter, angry person, and to no avail anyway. It would not change her father's conduct one bit, and while she knew this in her mind, her heart yet raged at the impossible situation into which her father had placed her. She shook her head sharply, dispelling the line of thought, and peered out the window.

The clouds, which had been threatening all morning, had blown elsewhere and now, though the branches on the trees swayed in the breeze, the sky was clear and blue. Nodding in acknowledgement to Michelle as she passed, she opened the door and made her way to the mercantile.

There, Missus MacFarland was in a dour mood, and she accepted the letter from Susannah with a frown.

"I cannot offer any guarantee that any post will reach its destination under the circumstances, you know."

"I am aware of that, and ask only that you dispatch it when you are able, by some means that seems most likely to survive the passage."

The shopkeeper's wife nodded and placed the letter in the packet atop the rest of the post with which she had been entrusted. Susannah could tell that it did not sit well with the woman to be unable to offer better assurances of the sanctity of the mails. Smiling tightly at the woman, she turned and opened the front door, given assistance by a gust that pushed it into her hand.

As she stepped through and pulled the door closed behind her, she nearly collided with her father, who was just arriving, looking pleased with himself. As that had been his normal countenance for these several weeks past, Susannah did not in particular mark it, but as she dodged walking into him, his face broke into a wide smile.

"I have happy news for you, my dear daughter, that may help to both take your mind off of the cares of our position under the threat of the rebellious raiders, and provide some balm for the discomfort that I have noticed in your regard for Miss Vincent and myself."

She stopped and raised a single eyebrow by way of reply.

He plunged on, his eyes fairly dancing in delight. "Alma has agreed to join me in matrimony, and to become your mother, and to make us a proper home all together."

Susannah blinked in surprise and took a deep

breath, giving herself a moment to let the news absorb into her mind, as a slow liquor in her gut might do.

All these years of wishing that she had a mother, someone to rock her to sleep, to smooth her hair back as she cried over a meaningless slight, someone to give advice and listen to her girlish ideas of the world, and like this, those wishes were... answered? A mother? Why, she had hardly any use for such a figure now, being nearly of age to strike out on her own, indeed, to consider the possibility of beginning a family herself.

When she could trust herself to speak, she asked, "When will the happy event take place, and will we offer notices to the invading forces as well to our friends and neighbors?"

Her father frowned at her tone and replied, "We shall dispense with the formality of publishing the banns, and have the minister join us in a simple ceremony with only our families." He colored slightly, adding, "I am aware that our conduct has not been entirely... correct, and as I am previously married, I should not want to make so much of a fuss over it."

"What of Michelle? Will we turn her out in thanks for her faithful and diligent service?"

"My dear daughter, I am afraid that we must." He looked abashedly at the ground for a moment, and then met her eyes. "I have suffered some not inconsequential reverses in relation to the depredations of the rebels who harry our shores. We are not so prosperous as we once were. Indeed, in addition to releasing Michelle to some other service, we will reduce our expenses by closing up the house and returning it to our landlord, and remove ourselves to your new mother's home."

She looked at him, aghast. "Could it be that you might better have weathered those reverses, were you not entirely consumed with an inappropriate and unsavory dalliance with that woman? In your eagerness to fill the empty place in your heart, you have destroyed our happy life together as father and daughter. I have tolerated your behavior without comment, thinking it just a reaction to the shocks of the past months, but this is a path too far." She stepped past him, willing her angry tears to stay their course until she should escape his presence.

He called after her, "Susannah, wait—there is one other thing. Your new mother is with child. You are to have a new sibling." She froze for a moment, and then shook her head angrily and continued to walk away without acknowledging this last cannonball through the crumbling walls that had surrounded her once comfortable and happy life.

Chapter 10

2nd December

My Dear Sister Susannah

Both of your Letters of this Summer have just this very Day reached my Hand, and I read them with Great Interest, being both Shocked and Comforted by your kind Company in my time of Grief. Matters continue in their Martial and Grave progression toward what End none can even hazard a Guess. All the Country around is alive with Intrigues and Conflicts, and the Trade has been all but Ceased, outside of a few Smugglers, but no Honest Man wishes to conduct business with such Ruffians. Acts of Intimidation and Violence against those who may still be counted among the King's Loyal Men have continued and even Escalated, including a Desecration which I am sad to report to you. Your former House, though Secured with care and unstinting Effort, has been Ransacked and Burnt, with none willing to fly to its Preservation once the Flames were kindled. Neither have any been willing to Seriously Inquire as to the Cause of the conflagration. What with all of these Troubles, I have begged my Father to remove us to join you in Nova-Scotia, but he maintains that our Position here is both Safe and Wholesome. The evidence of my own Eyes, in combination with the Dark Rumours which I hear Daily, convince me that he is Deluding himself, for what *cause I do not know. Oh, how I long for the silly Problems that we thought so Serious in our Departed Youth! Our fates were sunnier in those Days than we could Comprehend—and I fear for any Future vantage-point from which these present days may look so Favourable. We cower here, awaiting the next Stroke, insensible of where it may Fall, yet none the less certain of its Approach. This is no way for decent Christian peoples to treat with one another, and I pray constantly that our Vile Enemies may either see the non-sense of their Demands, or else fall in Utter Defeat, and by either means leave us to return to the Happy Conditions of Peace and Prosperity which obtained throughout the Land before they commenced their Disturbance of our Situation. I am Absent of advice to offer in the matter of your Papa's conduct, aside from the Observation that the terrible Disruptions of this age are likely to cause Good Men to fall to Regrettable Actions. Remember his Sacrifices to keep you in Safety, and try to find room in your generous Heart for some hint of the forgiveness that is our Birthright. As all is dear, and paper no less so than ever, I shall conclude this letter now, but know that I remain, now as ever,*

> *Your Sister in Grief and Worry,*
> *Emma*

After she finished reading it, Susannah held the letter to her heart for a moment, tears leaking from her eyes. The loss of the home she had known before her father had removed her to this place should not have caused her such pain, she knew, but it was yet another hammer-fall in so long a sequence as it might take a workman to drive a great spike into an oaken bole.

She carefully folded the letter and slipped it into

the compartment in her writing-box where she had secured the others. Composing herself, she turned back to the hearth, where her step-mother stood, slowly stirring a pot, her free hand caressing the belly which just barely showed the child growing within.

She looked up from the pot to Susannah, and noticed that the girl's eyes were bright with tears. "What is the matter, dear girl? More sad news from your friends?"

Susannah shook her head and scowled at her inability to conceal her heart from this woman. "It is nothing of import," she said. "Just that the war goes badly, which is no news." She did not wish to share more with this interloper in her life, and though a part of her burned with shame for how she was treating the gentle healer, she could not seem to overcome her anger at the woman—and her own father—for the unwanted changes their actions had wrought on her life.

"I should like to go out and visit with friends, if that does not hinder your plans for the afternoon?" Even if her heart raged at the woman, Susannah felt that she could at the very least reflect the civility of her upbringing.

Her step-mother considered for a moment, and then said, "Have you attended to the tasks that I asked of you this morning?"

"All save for fetching the wood from the shed. I will do that immediately."

"Thank you. Once that is done, you may go, but do listen sharp for any alarm that may be raised, and do not interfere with the rounds of the militia as they drill."

Susannah sighed in spite of herself. "Yes, Mother," she said, unable to keep the irritation out of her tone. Did she think that the same admonitions repeated every day would somehow correct a deficit in attention or behavior, if it had even been manifest to begin with? She resented, too, that her father had insisted without any allowance for her own preference, that Susannah call his wife her "Mother" as soon as the marriage was consecrated.

Shrugging her bearskin coat on and buttoning it against the wind that moaned through the house, she pushed her way through the door out into the blustery day. A few sullen snowflakes spat out of the sky, matching Susannah's mood as she stomped out to the shed to retrieve wood for the fire.

As she pulled wood from the pile under the rude shelter of the shed's tilted roof, she looked back at the house. It was far smaller than the house lost to fire and ransack, and even smaller than their first home in this town, but it was comfortable enough, though it offered little privacy. The walls were not so tight against the wind as she would have liked, either, but her father had promised to have that attended to just as soon as finances permitted.

As usual, he was off at the government office today, seeking compensation for a shipment which the Royal Navy had failed to adequately protect. He believed that law and custom was on his side, and that he would soon prevail in his claim, but so far, the Crown's representatives here had seemed powerless to make his losses whole.

Bringing in a large armload of wood, Susannah used her elbow to work the latch and pushed the door open with her hip. Setting it down by the hearth, she peered curiously over her step-mother's shoulder to see what was in the pot. Wrinkling her nose, she asked, "Onion soup again?"

"Yes, Susannah. I know it is not your favorite

meal, but supplies are most difficult to come by in the disruption of the trade. We are fortunate that Quebec has been able to send us some essentials again, but their attention has been elsewhere, even with the American siege of that city lifted. Montreal remains in enemy hands, and your father tells me that every ship that reaches our docks must first run a gauntlet of privateers and enemy patrols."

Susannah sighed again. It used to be that her father would discuss such matters with her, but since his marriage, he instead shared all with his wife, and she had to count herself fortunate to learn of his views second hand through her.

It also used to be that Michelle could find some way to vary their diet, even when provisions were dear, but her new step-mother's skills at the hearth seemed to turn more in the direction of disgusting draughts and less in the direction of appetizing cuisine. Not for the first time, Susannah found herself wishing that she had availed herself of the chance to learn more about the skills of the kitchen from the serving-girl, before that opportunity had passed.

"I understand, Mother. Perhaps I will find someone in town willing to part with a bit of salted meat at a price not too dear to bear, and we can have a stew on the morrow?"

"If you can, that would be most welcome," her step-mother replied. "Do not be disappointed, however, if you cannot. I have been thinking for some time that the old barred hen might have passed her prime as a layer, and it may be time to send her to the stew-pot."

Susannah frowned, feeling suddenly guilty. She did not want to be the cause of the animal's early demise, just because she was tired of smelling of onion. She hurried to say, "I do not think that will be needful, and while that hen may not be laying so much as she once did, she does a valuable service in keeping her juniors in order"

Her step-mother chuckled, a gentle, warm sound, and said, "Very well, I shall spare her for the moment, though you must appreciate that she was raised for that eventual purpose." She smiled at her step-daughter's concern for the bird in question, and waved a hand at the door. "Go, then, and see what fortune you may find in trade and in visiting with your friends. Mind the patrols," she repeated, and Susannah rolled her eyes, after she had turned to open the door.

Now that she had grown more accustomed to moving about on the frozen ground, she found it comical that she had ever fallen and hurt herself. Her ankle still hurt when a storm was coming in, or she had walked too far afield, but she was now nearly as sure-footed in wintertime as anyone who had always lived here.

She hadn't gotten but a few dozen paces from her door, however, when she heard the bells of the church steeple pealing out a warning, followed momentarily by the distant boom that she had come to recognize as cannon fire. She grimaced and turned on her heel back for the house. Whether it were an attack on the town itself, or the warning of yet another raid further up the coast, she knew that her step-mother would be beside herself with worry until both her step-daughter and husband were under her roof.

Hurrying back to the door, she entered to find herself encircled immediately in an embrace. "Ah, Susannah, thank you for returning to my call. I did not think you could hear me over the wind. I need your help, as I have just discovered that I may be losing the baby."

Chapter II

Third Day of March,
anno domini Seventeen Seventy-Six

My Dearest Sister Emma,
    I sincerely hope that this letter finds you safe & well. We hear such frightful notices of events in the region around the fair town of Boston, held in security still by our brave men in Red. The anger of the rebellious portion of the population sent hither by our former brothers in New-England seems to grow daily stronger, & we have seen evidences of unrest even among those whom we counted as our staunchest friends. So much has changed since last I was able to post a letter to you. Of greatest import to my condition in this place was the sudden surprise marriage of my father to the healing-woman whom he had hired to provide care for my ankle following the accident which I suffered last Winter. While their illicit association had grown in the past months, it was the discovery that the former spinster was with child that precipitated a hasty exchange of nuptials, & our equally sudden removal from the house in which we had established ourselves upon arrival to this town, to the smaller but less expensive home that she here owns. So, after so many years of being raised by my father alone, I have now a mother, albeit an unlooked-for one. To further complicate our domestic situation, she suffered these weeks past of a miscarriage,

& so the immediate cause of so much upheaval was lost. Though I am affected by the grief that seizes her still, I am also moved by the knowledge that the lost babe would have been born to a world in turmoil & descent, instead of the proper birthright of a child consisting of a world in peace & good order. Alas, among those whose interests I had expected attached to the side of the King was that selfsame fine boy, Colin, whose company I had found so charming in the summer of this year past. Once the rebel depredations began upon our shores, though, he had to but voice a tolerance for their viewpoint—nay, even a multitude of points of agreement—and I was certain that it was right to break entirely with him. I am happy to report that he has since kept himself distant from me at all times, & will continue to do so, should he not like a thrashing at my Papa's hands. It is a bitter draught to swallow, though, worse than any that my new mother might prepare, & I regret the loss of his company extremely. Despite the happy failure of the American forces to penetrate the town of Quebec, & the fortuitous fall of their most effective military commander at the siege, we have here in Halifax laboured under martial law, intended to ensure that no accused spies may hide amongst us & transmit intelligences to our enemies. As matters grow more dire yet in your region, we have seen so many of our former neighbours come lately to these parts that I have been surprised to not count you & your father among their number to this point. But I know that your father has said that his business & family connexions overmatch the dangers of remaining, & so it is with only a faint hope that I examine the weary faces of those who arrive on each ship from Boston, hoping to again behold your visage in this life. We are under the careful

protection of our parents, however, & we must trust them to make the best decisions that they can for us, given the information that they have gathered, absorbed, & considered. Another line & I shall conclude this & entrust it to those who tell me that they can get the post through, regardless of the conditions of war which obtain across the miles which separate you from me. I pray daily for your safety, comfort, & deliverance from the evil deeds that stalk our country in this time. Until we shall write again, I am,

    Your Loving Sister,
    Susannah

Her father and step-mother's door remained firmly closed despite the sun having risen behind sullen clouds some hours earlier, and so Susannah did not seek permission before she left the small house for the mercantile and her tenuous access to the post. She made her way through the familiar roads, avoiding the worst of the slushy mud along the way. The weather had been uncharacteristically warm for several days, and the winter's icy grip seemed to be broken for another year.

Along the way, she greeted a few people, but there were many unfamiliar faces on the roads. Had she once looked so bewildered and lost, her expression reflecting such a mixture of gratitude for deliverance from even more precarious surrounds and anxiety over the unknown dangers of a new locale? She lacked the boldness to approach these newcomers and offer them assurances of their safety—and indeed, with the constant raids and abuses of the rebels against the supply-ships and farmsteads of this area, no such assurance would be meaningful—but she tried to at least greet them with friendlier smiles than she remembered having been offered in her first days here.

When she arrived at the mercantile, she greeted the shopkeeper, "Good morning, Mister MacFarland. How fare you in these warm days?"

MacFarland shrugged in his characteristically underspoken manner and replied, "I remain on the right side of the grave, so I fare better than some."

She smiled in response to his familiar witticism, and gestured toward the house portion of the structure. "Missus MacFarland is well?"

"Aye, and the wee bairns," he said, letting his heavy birth accent show for a moment, and then returning to the relatively unaccented speech he had learned to adopt for the sake of business among the mixed population of the colony. "She's been fairly bursting to share the latest gossip with you, though, so why don't you go on in and pay her a visit?"

"Thank you, Mister MacFarland, I shall do so without further delay. Before I forget, though, I have another letter for my dear friend in Massachusetts, if you can attempt to dispatch it for conveyance to what posts may be running in these days?"

"As always, Miss Mills," he said gravely as he accepted the letter from her hand. "So long as you have not inscribed any matters of military intelligence herein, there should be no reason that it will not be passed through for delivery."

She smiled in response. "I cannot imagine that I possess any information that might be of interest to the martial mind, and if I have by some accident included such intelligences within my correspondence, I should hope to be forgiven my lapse."

He nodded and said, "Aye, you might not come

under prosecution, but your letter would suffer for the interrogation, most likely to its destruction. 'Tis a risk all correspondence must run in these days, of course."

"I know this well, and I count myself fortunate for every missive that is delivered, either from my hand or to it. Thank you for your kindness in forwarding this letter on to its fate, whatever that may be."

She dipped slightly in formal farewell and passed through the door into the residence, as he said, "'Tis a pleasure to be of service, Miss Mills."

Entering the kitchen, she called out, "Missus MacFarland, 'tis your friend Susannah, and I am given to understand that you have some matters to discuss with me?"

From the back room, she heard the shopkeeper's wife call back, "Yes, my dear—I'll be right out, just make yourself at home." Susannah took a seat on the bench at the kitchen table and waited, looking around the familiar room.

The utensils hung by the hearth differed little from those which graced her own kitchen, though the few that they had brought with them from home provided a stark contrast with the quality of those that had originally been in her new step-mother's use.

The great cookpot, of course, and the heavy spider had been too massive to bring with them, but her father had gathered up some of his mother's prized hand tools, as well as a couple of good knives, and between it all, their kitchen was complete enough.

Susannah suffered another pang of sadness as she pondered the fate of the kitchen implements left behind. They either occupied the hearth of some wretched despoiler and thief, or else they were lost in the ruins of the burnt house. She shook her head to dispel this somber line of thought, just as Missus MacFarland bustled into the room, still knotting up the laces on her stays.

She rushed up to Susannah and embraced her, saying, "It is so good to see you, my dear, and looking so spry and fine on this lovely spring day!"

Susannah smiled at the effusive woman and replied, "You are in fine fettle today, Missus MacFarland. What has you in such a rush of joy?"

The woman smiled and gave Susannah a sideways look. "Well, I just thought that you would want to hear it first from a friend, but your old walking-companion Colin McRae, has just announced his engagement to the daughter of one of those Yorkshiremen—a girl I think you know well, name of Michelle Stayton?"

Suannah controlled herself, but she felt her face grow hot for a moment before she replied, as casually as she could, "Ah, is that so? I am so happy for them both, though I must wonder how the daughter of a fiercely loyal King's Man of Yorkshire and a boy who sympathizes with our devilish attackers will resolve those differences."

Missus MacFarland shrugged and said, "Not all view the world through the same set of experiences you have passed through, my dear. I do hope that this news does not cause you any undue distress."

Susannah feigned unconcern and replied, "None in particular, no." She glanced through the window and noticed that the morning had darkened under a threatening bank of clouds. "I had best be off, though, lest the weather break as I walk, and I should get entirely soaked to the skin."

Missus MacFarland gathered her in for another large, comfortable embrace, and said, "You are right, of course. You'll be wanting to get home and safe in your bed before the rain falls."

Nodding, Susannah returned the embrace, and then excused herself through the front door, not wanting to pass again through the public space of the shop. She took a little-used road home, preferring solitude to the company of strangers or worse yet, acquaintances. Missus MacFarland was right—it was a good day to spend snug in a warm bed.

Susannah did not make it more than halfway home, though, before the first icy droplets fell from the sky to mingle with the hot tears that already flowed down her cheeks.

Chapter 12

20th May, 1776

My Dear Sister Susannah,

Without I have yet received a Reply to my last letter to you, I still desired to offer you immediate Assurances of my Safety, although I fear that we may now never again enjoy each others' Society in this world, with the Events that have lately transpired in Boston-Town. The defenders of our last secure Outpost in this violently convulsed Colony have been forced under threat of utter Destruction to quit their positions in that City, leaving the King's Men completely exposed to any horrors that the Rebels may wish to visit upon our Persons or Souls. Although many of the Loyalists of this region have now followed the Wise Example of your father in departing these shores for the country around your fair Town, my own Father has steadfastly Refused, citing the inherent Humanity of our former brothers, despite my desperate Pleas to reconsider his inflexible position. I cannot credit his faith in the Rebel's respect for the boundaries of Decent conduct, given the many instances of their Depravity. Just last month, they seized up a man whom they accused of Espionage, and subjected him to the Barbarous act that they call "smoking," wherein they push their unfortunate Victim into the throat of his own chimney, and then set a Fire about his feet, so that he has no option but *to inhale the unhealthful Fumes of the same. Many such sad subjects of such Treatment are pulled from their Predicament lifeless, and no efforts on their behalf are sufficient to restore them. I only pray they these Monstrous Acts are not visited upon my own Family, tho my Father assures me that his willingness to accede to any demand for an Oath that they may demand of him will suffice to Insulate us from the hazards of this Age. I have watched with Wretched Sadness as prominent and upright Families of this town and those nearby, many of whose Names will be as familiar to you as my own, have formed a Procession passing through the District as they seek the relative safety of the Sea and the happier Prospects that lie that way, through what Hardships I may only imagine. The wickedness of our former friends and Neighbours continues to astound me with every report that reaches my ears. What they Pursue, all People whose Opinions I value say ought to have been addressed through force of arguments, and not through taking up Arms and committing divers Cruel Acts. Send my greetings to any Friends we share who might safely reach the shores of your new Town, and know that I am with you in the cares of my Heart, despite the conspiracy of Events that has interrupted our happy Friendship. Until I shall again read the Thoughts you set down with your pen, I remain,*

> *Your Devoted Sister,*
> *Emma*

Susannah had not needed Emma's letter to know that calamity had befallen the Crown's forces in Boston, as the town and all the countryside around was choked with those who had sought refuge from the depredations of the rebels. Many had escaped with little but the clothes on their backs, or, if they had tried to bring anything of greater value, they had been stripped of it as a condition of their flight with the British forces.

The crimson coats of the King's regulars drilled daily now in various open spaces in and around the town, although they were forced to give way to temporary accommodations for the sad and bewildered refugees of Boston-Town and its surrounding countryside. In pursuit of information, as well as any bit of corn-flour that might remain in their stores, Susannah went to the mercantile one afternoon a few days after Emma's letter had arrived.

When she arrived, she found the shopkeeper's wife scowling over an account at the till. "Good day to you, Miss Susannah," she called out in greeting as the girl entered the shop.

Susannah replied, "And to you, Missus MacFarland. What news of the day?"

The woman snorted and said, "We are beset with more than we can feed and less with which to make the attempt, the same as the last time you visited this establishment."

"I had cherished the hope that you may have received some supplies with all the shipping that I have seen pass through."

"Nay, they all bear yet more passengers, save for a few which carry goods and supplies meant for the exclusive use of the military men here gathered."

"If the numbers who gathered here are any indication," Susannah retorted, "then the districts around Boston itself must be very nearly empty."

"I know not how many might remain, but 'tis sure that they overrun this place, and likely London and the Indies as well."

Susannah shook her head, her brow furrowing. "How awful must conditions truly be in our rebellious colonies, if so many are willing to risk the voyage, what with the Americans' privateers and what naval forces they can muster adding to the normal perils of such travel."

"I fear that we can know only the barest of details from this remove, my dear girl. We are most certainly the happier for it, too."

Susannah grimaced by way of agreement, and asked, "So you have no corn-flour, then? Nor any molasses? My Papa was hoping for a hasty pudding today, to tempt Mother's palate."

The shopkeeper's wife scowled in thought for a moment, and then said, "I might have some corn-flour in the bottom of a barrel in the store-room, but I cannot warrant that it is free of pests. As for molasses, that is something that I do still have a fair supply of, though some of the more enterprising young soldiers are threatening to consume all of that now, too, as they have discovered a method for turning it into a sorry sort of ale."

She shook her head, rolling her eyes in a gesture that Susannah knew all too well. "Young men and their appetite for any sort of liquor that might help them to pass the day through. One would think that their quartermasters would fetch along enough rum to keep the men satisfied, but I have yet to see it happen."

Looking back to Susannah, she said, "Wait here, and I'll fetch your corn-flour. The molasses you can draw from the barrel over there," and she pointed to a cask laid on its side, with a gummed-looking spigot inserted into the bung. "You'll be needing a crock for that, as well?"

Susannah nodded, and said, "I must confess that I had not hoped to find that you yet had molasses available, and so I did not prepare myself for that possibility."

"Well, you know where they are, so help yourself, and I shall add it to your account." She bustled into the store-room, while Susannah fetched a lidded crock from the shelf, carried it over to sit beneath the spigot, removed and set aside the lid, and then gingerly reached out to turn the handle on the spigot. As she anticipated, it was sticky in the extreme, and stiff to turn.

By the time she had coaxed a thick, sullen stream of the dark molasses to begin flowing into the crock, both hands were blackened and her fingers felt tacky as she brushed them against one another while she watched the crock filling. Missus MacFarland returned from the store-room with a paper-wrapped package of flour, and as Susannah looked up at her, she saw the door open, and Colin stepped inside.

The shopkeeper's wife looked from one of them to the other and then said hurriedly, "I'll just check in the store-room for that other item you were wanting, Miss Susannah. Won't be but a few minutes." She set down the package and rushed out of sight again.

Left alone with him, Susannah could not help but notice that he looked hale, and had, perhaps, even grown taller and stronger-looking than before. She was acutely aware that she was in her old second-best gown, and that her hair was only barely controlled under her cap and kerchief. She had anticipated just dropping by the mercantile this day, and not having to contend with an encounter with Colin.

Colin looked away sheepishly for a moment, and then raised his eyes to meet Susannah's gaze. He asked quietly, "How have you been, Susannah?"

She answered, as steadily as she could, "I've been busy." She surreptitiously started to wipe her hands on her apron, but it only stuck to them, and she quickly balled them up by her side. "My parents have had much for me to do, and my studies have also consumed me."

"I see," he replied, and fell into an awkward silence.

Susannah was determined not to let him escape the issue that she knew he wanted desperately to avoid. "How go your preparations for your wedding?"

He flushed scarlet, and stammered, "Well, uh, Michelle is, erm, handling most all of those… details."

Her gaze bored into his eyes as she replied without mercy, "I imagine that you are looking forward to enjoying the experience of her skills in the kitchen… and elsewhere."

He turned even brighter red before replying, "I have not had occasion to sample her cooking, as we spend most of our time together assisting her father on his farm. With the arrival of so many more mouths to feed in our community, it is more crucial than ever that we have a bountiful harvest."

He gasped then, and pointed behind her, where the molasses had overrun the sides of the crockery, and was spreading in a tarry pool toward her skirts. She whirled and crouched to force the spigot shut, noting with mounting fury that she had thereby dipped nearly the entire hem of her petticoat into the sticky molasses.

When she turned back around, her eyes flashing with rage, she found that Colin had made good his escape, and Missus MacFarland had returned from the store-room, and stood looking at Susannah and the sticky catastrophe spreading around her on the floorboards, wincing in sympathetic horror at the girl's humiliation.

Chapter 13

20th July, 1776

My Precious Sister Susannah,
 I will pray to not be the first bearer of the Vicious News, but I have read lately in the news-papers of this Unfaithful Colony that the self-styled Representatives of this and the other Rebelling Colonies have gathered together in that wretched town of Philadelphia and have jointly Declared for Independence. Shall we then be separated not only by the cruelty of War, but by an inimical Frontier, as well? I weep for the ill Fortune that so threatens us. At present, now that the British forces have completed their Evacuation of Boston, and the majority of the Loyalists hereabouts have followed them, a strange calm has descended upon the country around here. The rebels still patrol about, and from time to time, they accost and threaten those of us who are suspected of loyalty to the King, but they are largely Engaged elsewhere, and my Family and I are for the most part Safe and Secure. The chief effect of the rebellious Feeling in these parts is in regard to the trade, which is nearly entirely Choked Off. The rebels have announced that the Boston Port is open to trade with all Nations save our own Britain, but it is a brave crew indeed that will hazard the Ire of the Royal Navy. Through some means of conveyance, I have, however, received your latest Letter, which leaves me feeling Low and Sad on

your account. I pray that your Especial Friend will come to his Senses and see that not only is his chosen Cause a foolish one, but that he has forsaken a True Heart in its favour. And if he shall not, then oh, wicked boy! I shall spit upon the Ground where he walks (if only in my thoughts, as we now seem to be past all Hope of sharing a common Country in these woeful days). He cannot be the only Prospect that you shall find, however, and our Loss of fine, eligible young men is your Gain, if you take my meaning clear. Alas for we left Behind here, but take heart for your Potentialities. I do hope that your step-mother has recovered her health, and that your father has returned to his Wits now that the Urgency of the moment has passed, and that he has again been the Wise Counselor to his daughter. 'Twould be a Pity and a shame for his Wise Choice in bringing you thence to be Undone by short-lived Passion. You are in my Thoughts constantly, and I await with eagerness every Visitor to these Parts, in the hope that he may carry another of your Correspondences. Without regard for the sad or joyful News they contain, they serve to remind me that the World beyond these embattled Parts is still a place where Martial matters are not Supreme in our lives, and where Loyal Subjects of HRH the King need not surrender both their Arms and their Dignity in order to be suffered merely to Eke out a bare existence. It would be too much for me to pray to the Author of the World that our former brothers should return to their Senses and their Allegiance to their Sovereign, but I will permit myself to Dream that this may yet come to pass, through what Means I cannot imagine. I remain your

    Devoted Sister,
    Emma

The streets of the town had been not only awash in the refugees who had continued to pour out of the rebellious colonies, but abuzz with discussions of their latest affront to the King. Susannah, having learned that Colin was away for the summer at his prospective father-in-law's farm, dared venture out to the mercantile again, where she took a place at the edge of the throng that was discoursing upon the news on the front step.

"It is not entirely unreasonable," one short man with flaming red hair and a pronounced brogue was saying, "that these Colonists should take up their grievances against the King by both words and deeds, particularly when the Parliament seems so ill-humored in the question of considering their petitions."

There was a grumble from several in the crowd, and he held up his hands, saying, "Now hear me out. I do not defend their rebellious acts, nor the violence that they have visited upon the King's loyal men across the Colonies. However, without defending those acts, we can acknowledge that their claim for relief is not wholly without merit."

A black-haired man with a coarse accent interrupted the speaker, his fury getting the better of him. "But—independence? That ought be the last resort, after all other possibilities have been exhausted, rather than their reaction at the first resistance to their uncivil and extreme demands. There can be no reconciliation now with these rebels, until they all shall dance on the hangman's knot."

Several of the men in the crowd nodded in agreement, and their growl of approval was a chilling sound. Susannah wondered where they would draw the line between rebel and Tory, and the fate that they would visit upon even someone such as Colin, with his mere expressions of approval of the American cause, or even Emma's family, with their determination to stay in the rebel-held territory.

Someone else gave voice to this thought nearly as soon as it had formed in her mind, though, his voice carrying the distinctive sound of a Yorkshireman's accent. "Who is to decide whether a given man is a foul turncoat against the King, or was merely driven to it by circumstance or by being ill-informed? 'Tis all well and good to speak blithely of the hangman's rope, but if you had ever seen a line of sad corpses so treated, you would not be so swift to call for its wide application."

A few mutters of "Hear, hear," and the man continued, "I will be second to no man in my loyalty to the Crown for their excessive generosity in both securing these lands to us, and in sharing them so freely with we who are newly-come to these shores. However, I should rather prefer to think of these rebels as brothers astray from their true path in this life, and to treat with them such that they will desire to return to the blessings of the King's protection."

The angry man's voice replied tightly, "If you have read their utterances, you would know that there is no opening to treat with them—they leave no room for compromise and discussion. Why, some of them have gone so far as to question whether any nation ever needed a King at all, and they have advocated that the masses shall rule in all matters."

He paused to drink from the mug he held in his hand, and Susannah noticed that he seemed to be sweating far in excess of what the heat of the day justified. He continued, "Why, the mob is fully in control of some of their territories. I am recently escaped from Massachusetts Colony, where huge mobs are nightly going through the countryside with torches alight, and firing the homes of all they suspect of any petty offense, hanging the men and raping the daughters, without any regard for either decency or the proper rule of law over the passions."

Susannah frowned and spoke, hesitantly, "I have just today received a letter from my dear friend in that Colony, and while she says that trade is sorely interrupted, and those few Loyalists still remaining there are subject to certain harassments, she did not write of any such actions."

Another man spoke up, picking up the thread of her comments, "I do not think that we need exaggerate the ill-mannered actions of our foes in order to support the continued energetic opposition to their goals."

The black-haired man glared at Susannah, but kept his counsel as the discussion shifted back to the details of the Declaration of Independence, which had been posted and remained, though defaced, after its publication in the Gazette the prior week.

Feeling uncomfortable under the unfriendly gaze of the angry man whose argument she had upset, Susannah made her way past the crowd and into the shop, where Mister MacFarland stood at the till, holding court there with a much smaller crowd, but rehearsing many of the same arguments she had already heard outside.

She examined the items behind the counter for a while, until he took notice of her presence and called out, "Good day to you, young Miss Mills. I trust that matters are tolerably well with you?"

She nodded politely and replied, "I am just here after some hartshorn, should you happen to have any. My step-mother desired it, though whether for a dish or a draught, she did not say."

The shop keeper's brow wrinkled briefly in thought, and he said after a moment, "I do not think that I have any, no, but I may be able to lay hands on some in a few days' time. 'Tis not so difficult to find someone with a small supply laid by in these parts, and it is common enough to not be too terrible dear."

Susannah nodded, saying, "I shall convey that advice to her, and will return in a few days if not sooner. I tarried too long at the notice-board, and should return home."

"Very well, then, I look forward to your return," he said. She went to the door and smiled in reply to his friendly wave of farewell.

Outside, she blinked a couple of times in the bright midday sun, and adjusted her bonnet to shield her eyes somewhat. The crowd on the front step had gotten no quieter in her absence, and the black-haired man was engaged in an intense discussion with three other men, the redness of his face belying the content of his mug.

Susannah turned away and walked toward home, shaking her head to herself. Rum made men's tongues looser than they ordinarily might be, but most chose to imbibe in moderation, and without giving their unfenced opinions room to roam the countryside.

Still lost in thought about the dangers of strong drink, she did not at first hear the voice calling her name. The young man repeated more loudly, "Susannah Mills? Late of Massachusetts? Is it really you?"

She turned to see a well-dressed man, perhaps a few years her senior, waving to her from the other side of the street. Her mouth gaped in recognition as she flew to him, and stopping short, bowed her head courteously and offered her hand to him. "Roger Black, it is an unexpected pleasure to behold you in these streets."

He took her hand, bowed over it, and replied, pulling her into an embrace, "You ridiculous girl, greeting me as though I were a stranger at your door. 'Tis good to see you here, as well. Your father is also in these parts, I take it?"

She returned the embrace loosely, aware that propriety barred her from excess effusion, and then stepped back. "Indeed he does, and though he may not be in a state to receive guests at the moment, I would be most glad to remember you to him, and arrange for a proper welcome to you."

He replied, "That would be most gratefully received, as I am just arrived on these shores, and a friendly face would do me much good. The resumption of a happy combination with my mentor would be a comfort, also." He looked thoughtful for a moment, and then added, "I have some opportunities upon which I would value his advice, as well."

Susannah thought furiously for a moment, and then decided that she could risk extending an invitation. "Should you care to dine with us on the morrow, perhaps?"

He tilted his head graciously and replied, "It would be a great honor." He smiled at her, and she thought she detected in his eyes something more than merely the joy of re-establishing contact with the family of the man for whom he had worked as a youth. There was a speculative aspect to his gaze for just a moment, but he broke eye contact and the moment passed as he continued, "Shall I call on him at mid-day tomorrow, then?"

"That would be most welcome, I am certain. We

may be found in the small house at the corner where this street ends." She pointed in the right direction, and he nodded in acknowledgement and again bowed over her hand.

She felt a strange thrill pass up her arm as his mouth brushed just ever so briefly against her fingers, but then he rose again and said, "Please tell your father that I am most grateful for the happenstance that brings me again to his door. I am eager to resume our friendship." With that odd smile returning to his face, he added, "Until tomorrow, Susannah," then turned on his heel and was gone up the street.

Chapter 14

September the Seventeenth,
anno domini Seventeen Seventy-Six

My Dear Sister Emma,
I hope fervently that you continue to enjoy some measure of peace & safety. The rumours that are given as true gospel about the conditions which obtain across the whole of the rebellious territory are lurid & alarming in the extreme, but with the assurances of your continued communications, I have been able to set aside the concerns that these tales might otherwise raise in my mind. Events here continue to make the mind whirl. Troops have arrived from & departed for divers theaters in the war, & some few have remained behind & have commenced construction of a new fort to the South of town proper, for our defence. At the same time, though it would seem madness to so engage in the face of so many seasoned & disciplined men of the King's army, the air is here filled with word of intrigues & plots, & I can only imagine what tales you are hearing of events & conditions here. We are particularly alarmed by the stronghold of New-England men in the vicinity of the former fort at the St. John river, who have declared that they will conduct no business with those who maintain loyalty to the King. The military garrison here does not seem inclined to dispense with this threat, & in truth, some of those who have made

the boldest statements against the King in public are all too happy to take our money in private. Without regard to these hazards, however large or small they may turn out to be, be assured yourself that we are hale & safe, & are working our way back to some semblance of prosperity—about which I shall write more presently. What reliable news we get from those locations at which the forces of the rebels & those of the King have come into direct conflict give us reason for cautious optimism. Despite their reputation for barbarous conduct upon the field of battle, we have developed an impression that they attempt good order—but fail at it often, to their disappointment & woe. On many occasions, it seems, our forces have stayed their hands out of mercy & to demonstrate good-will, in hopes of earning the same from their forces, & with an eye toward the day when they shall lay down their arms & treat with us again as brothers & countrymen. In particular, the accounts we have here had of the late action at New York appears to have embodied the best illustration of these principles, & it is to be hoped that the rebels elsewhere across the colonies shall take note & ponder the most reasonable terms of their surrender, that we may put this entire sorry affair behind us & resume our former happy condition as subjects of the Crown's dominion across all England & over the seas as well. Our domestic condition in this household is curiously altered by late events. Among those who took flight from the regions around Boston was one Roger Black, whom you & I knew slightly in his association with Papa's business dealings, & about whom we had occasion to remark on several occasions. He has busied himself during the months of this contest with locating reliable suppliers of various divers goods, both wholesome & necessary, to all concerned. His sources have remained constant throughout the disruptions of war & pestilence, & he has presented himself to my Papa in search of wisdom, advice, & introductions to the many men of commerce with whom Papa has previously had business associations. Thus combined, their connexions have enabled Papa to return to his business, which has helped him wonderfully in putting behind him the loss of both his son & his new wife's babe not yet born. With this sense of purpose, he seems a new man, & it is most wonderful to see. Mister Black is full of kindnesses toward my person, as well, which is most flattering & which has assisted me in putting behind me my own disappointments. Did I previously write to tell you of Colin's perfidy? I remember not, but in the event, he is now engaged to be wed to the girl whom he met when she tended our hearth during my recovery. It was a strange & disappointing reverse, & one which affected me more than I would have expected, given how little that boy & I had actually had to do with one another. Setting that sad episode aside, though, Mister Black is a most pleasing dinner companion, a fine conversationalist, & a subtle, but effective, flatterer. I know not where his intentions might lie, nor will I make so bold as to inquire directly, but I will instead enjoy them in the moment. Oh, listen to me prattling on about such things when there is a war on! The Governor has taken the extraordinary step of setting forth fixed prices for certain goods, & with the late addition of new residents in these parts, rents have doubled. We are fortunate that my step-mother is well established here, & that our home is not subject to the caprices of such shocks. Had we still been in our first house here, we should have been forced to give it up; as it is, that

selfsame structure now houses three families, so it is difficult for me to continue in any of my former resentment of having left it. I hope that this letter offers you some cheer in the continued time of difficulties. Despite all signs that it will presently be past, & that life will return to a more normal shape, that day is not yet here, & so I must restrain my enthusiasms. Eagerly awaiting word from you of equal improvement in your condition, I remain, as always,
Your Affectionate & Loving Sister,
Susannah

An early fall shower spattered the ground all about Susannah, but she could not bring herself to feel concerned by it. She had just enjoyed a most successful dinner with her father, step-mother and the ever-charming Mister Black, and even rain upon her evening chores could not dislodge her happy mood, and the lightness of her heart.

Though the table was sparsely supplied by the standards of a more plentiful time, Mister Black had been able to procure a small roast, and together with some closely-hoarded spices and sugar, with a liberal addition of fruits Susannah had bought from a woman who concealed her face, but who could not hide her New England accent, she had helped her step-mother to produce a triumphant pie, richly supplied with a thick and savory gravy, and accompanied by a small but rich pudding.

In all, as good as the food had been, the conversation about the table had been even more enjoyable. Susannah's step-mother had been in rare form, and her tales of healing the town's sick had all around the table laughing hysterically.

With a smile on her face, she spoke in her characteristic soft tones, a smile playing around the edges of her mouth as she began. "If you can imagine, this very prim and proper man, an upstanding member of the community, having to come to a woman healer, as no 'proper doctor,' as he put it, was available to physic him. And the condition for which he came to consult was a most delicate one, which I will not here name, out of respect both for the meal and for the innocence of my daughter's ears"—Susannah blushed—"but suffice to say that the examination was most intensely upsetting for us both."

She gave Susannah a doting smile and continued, "I did my best to conceal my true feelings in the matter, and to simply identify and prepare what poultice and draught I thought would best answer for it. Neither were pleasant courses of treatment, but he bore up under them without complaint. It was not long after that he sailed for England in shame, no closer to a cure than when I first saw him."

She paused for a moment and sipped at her tea. "Not two days later, his neighbor visited, and he was suffering the same malady. I questioned him quite closely and frankly, and learnt that the ailment that they shared came from the well that they shared. Once properly diagnosed, I was able to treat and cure it in a matter of days."

She shook her head ruefully. "I had, in fact, made an incorrect diagnosis of the first case, that his malady could not have come of the deed that I assumed of him, and further, that he was so possessed of a guilty conscience that he was willing to be physicked for an illness that he did not have."

Mister Black had begun to chuckle first, and

before long, they were all laughing aloud at the first man's mistaken treatment, and the assumptions under which he had tolerated it.

As their laughter began to subside, Susannah's step-mother said, "A case such as this comes to me not more than once every few years, but when it does, it resolves me to be better educated and more careful in my diagnoses, yet there is so much that is discovered every year, and so little of it is readily accessible."

Susannah's father suddenly got a thoughtful, distant look in his eyes, and he said, "It would be most helpful to you to have a subscription of the philosophical transactions of the Royal Society, would it not? I have heard it said that the greatest philosophers of any country present their findings therein, and that it is the repository of all important new discoveries in all the natural philosophies, including the arts of medicine."

His wife, flustered, said, "Why, yes, Richard, but that costs a great deal, even in London, and to have it posted all the way here—"

He waved away her objections, saying, "My dear, I shall shortly be able to spare you no expense that shall make you happier or more certain in the pursuit of your chosen field of endeavor. Our Mister Black and I are shortly to make our fortunes, and by that success, lift this entire family back to the station in which we ought to reside."

He smiled indulgently at his wife. "There is nothing wrong with this house, mind you. 'Tis a fine place for a woman alone, who has for so long made her way on the sweat of her own brow. As you are now supported by a loving husband, and we have the dependency of a daughter, though, it might be nice to make this a more fitting home to those conditions."

His wife smiled uncertainly back, and said, tentatively, "I have wished that there were a copy of the Royal Society's proceedings readily available, and you know that I have long dreamed of adding a new wing onto the western side of the house."

Her smile grew sunnier. "Do you really believe that your venture will succeed to such an extent, even with the restrictions that the government has put on what prices may be charged for common goods?"

Mister Black spoke up now. "I am quite certain of it. Most of the things that I have secured the purchase of are not even on the government's lists, and yet are quite dear to those people who have money still. Given how many of these selfsame people are either in government, or have the ear of those who are, there is little danger that our goods will find themselves on such lists."

He smiled broadly, and said, "Your husband's reputation as a fair and honest merchant, combined with the contacts I have developed, ensure that we cannot but enjoy the greatest of success. Once the rebels are defeated and peace returns to this nation, we will build on that success, such that it should not surprise me if your husband and I wind up being the wealthiest men in this town, nay, even the entire colony!"

He raised his mug, as though it were a fine glass that contained the proudest Champagne of France, and not a humble cider poured from a cask in the kitchen. "Let us drink to victory, to success, and to wealth."

Susannah's father seized his own mug and raised it, shouting, "Hear, hear!"

Susannah and her step-mother joined in the toast, and in drinking the King's health and the army's success, and the frustration of the enemy. By the time they were done toasting, the cask in the kitchen was noticeably lighter, and everyone around the table was quite jolly indeed.

When it was time for Mister Black to don his greatcoat and venture back to the apartment he had secured, Susannah accompanied him to the door while her father stayed in the kitchen to keep his wife company as she cleaned up after dinner.

At the door, he said to her, "'Tis good to see you smile without reservation again. You look more like the girl I recall from when I last worked with your father."

She smiled shyly and replied, "'Tis good to see my father in such spirits again, as well, and I can only credit your presence for that. Your arrival here was a blessing indeed."

He smiled back at her and put his hand on the latch. Before he opened it and rushed out into the blustery afternoon, though, he leaned down and brushed a quick kiss on her cheek, leaving Susannah with her mouth hanging open in stunned joy and her face blazing red as the door closed behind him.

Chapter 15

3rd November, 1776

My Dear and Blessed Sister Susannah,
    It was with great joy that I read your most recent Letter. It is clear to see that the great Author of the Universe has been listening to your Prayers, and has chosen to answer them in Glorious Fashion. I am sorry to hear that your kind and trusting Heart sustained such Wounds at the unworthy bidding of that Boy, whose name I shall never again utter but to Curse him. Your Involvement with Mister Black is intriguing to my mind, and I await your next missive with my Heart prepared for any manner of Joy that may be brought a person. Here, our situation is subject to continued Improvements. The rebel Washington—formerly a Colonel in the King's service, tho, they say, one much given to dourness and Error—is everywhere on the Run, and it can be only a matter of Time before he is brought to Justice, and his armies disbanded forever. We hear such dashing Notices of our General Howe's successes in the field, as well as his extreme Cleverness in detecting rebel Plots against him. He has captured and Hanged several rebel Spies of late, discovering their Plans and Subterfuges as though guided by the Hand of Divine Providence itself. Upon reflection, I cannot think of any Events that have favoured the Rebels in all these months since last I set pen to paper for the Purpose of

*addressing you. I only hope that my next letter will contain the
Happy News of the capture of the Leaders of this rebellion, and
the details of the Justice meted out to them each in turn. The
violence that they have here done upon our Society makes the
Gallows a cheap price for them to pay. Though the Colony is a
staunchly rebel Territory, we are strangely at Peace in our daily
Affairs, as the armies maneuver and Fight in places distant,
and the men who are so Inclined are not here, but are there. It
is a strange and uncomfortable Peace, but I do not resent it for
its Oddity. Affairs have returned to a sense of Normalcy, to the
point where I have even had Callers again. It seems a disloyal
thing to do after your Brother's tragic loss, but they will not be
dissuaded, and I must offer them at least the Appearance of a
polite reception. None have yet succeeded in turning my head,
but my Father is desirous that I should continue in the practise.
In truth, it does me some Good to be flattered, even if it does not
yet reach my Heart. If that should change, you shall be the First
to whom I confide. I am most eager for further Word of the
ongoing improvements to your Situation! Until I shall again
hear from you, I remain,*

> *Your Devoted Sister,*
> *Emma*

As the snow piled up outside, and the meager fire
in the hearth popped and sighed, Susannah resisted the
urge to crumple the letter and toss it into the flames.
Instead, she dutifully folded it and put it with the rest,
in the tightly-packed writing box. She had no appetite
to reply just now, and could not anticipate when she
might.

While she sat despondent before the hearth, her

step-mother was again taken to her bed, and her father had trudged out to town, doubtless with the object of attempting yet again to repair his shattered reputation.

The first sign of trouble was a wild rumor that had spread through the town one cold day the prior month. A cutter had appeared at the docks, bearing an officer who had brought word of a concerted rebel attack on the fort at Cumberland, with the aim of further emboldening the Whiggish settlers to the east of town, destroying the major means of defense against a full-scale invasion, and gathering up an even greater force to bring against the town itself, and the officials of the government who resided there.

These tales seemed too far-fetched to be true, but shortly after the cutter's arrival, the Royal Marines mustered and marched in haste out of town, and observers reported that they had been seen to board a ship and depart under a full press of sail toward Cumberland.

When the Marines returned, the truth of the engagement began to be known around town. Upon their arrival at the fort—which had indeed been under siege—they had routed the rebel forces, some of whom had been invaders from Massachusetts and points along the coast on the way.

The rebellious locals had surrendered to the King's mercy, and had been paroled, after hard questioning, but most of the invaders among the rebel besiegers of the fort had faded away with their Indian guides, and had disappeared into the forested inland. A detachment still pursued them, but the opinion around town was that the weather and terrain would soon bring the troublemakers to a higher justice than could be handed out by the Marines or the judiciary.

All of this was distressing enough, but at the time of the attack, Mister Black had been out traveling to the suppliers with whom he had made arrangements, taking deliveries of goods from them, with promise of payment upon delivery to Halifax, so as to conserve what capital the partners had, until the goods should be sold at market there, which would then provide ample funds to both repay the suppliers and purchase the next round of goods.

Susannah knew enough to understand that such an arrangement would have been unheard of, particularly in light of the chances of war, except that her father's good reputation acted as a guarantee to all who knew him from his trade in Massachusetts. The suppliers felt secure in making such arrangements with him, against the promise of higher prices than they might otherwise have gotten for their goods, knowing that the ongoing conflict might possibly reach into their region, even though it had so far been a distant threat.

With the attack on the fort at Cumberland, that threat had been realized, with rebel forces gathering and marauding along the coast as they went. It was in this context that Mister Black—and a ship laden with expensive goods—had vanished, leaving no trace—and no answers to the pressing questions of both the heart and the purse.

Chapter 16

2nd February, 1777

My Dear Sister Emma,

I am heartbroken & bereft. Our Mister Black is gone, by all appearances a victim of the recent plot by the rebels to defeat this Colony by force of arms, & so add a Fourteenth to their disloyal number of States. By the will of Providence, that scheme was frustrated, but at what cost we cannot yet fully know. It was a trifling matter, as military adventures may be rated, but it has utterly upended both our community & home. Roger's loss has ruined Papa, both for the upset to our plans & aspirations, & by the merely financial reverses that the fortunes of war have yet again laid upon him. It was very good to dream of escaping this dreary material poverty & returning to our accustomed prosperity, but it is somehow all the harder to remain at this low station in life after the prospect of a higher was, for a while, held out before us like a promise, now violated. We are fortunate—no warlike violence has been visited upon us (outside of Mister Black's uncertain, but doubtless tragic, fate), we continue to eat, & walk, & breathe for a while yet, but still it is impossible to evade the sense that we are worse-off now than we were before, tho our condition is largely unchanged. Unrequited hope is more difficult to bear than even its complete absence would be. I do hope that you are correct in

*your last letter, & that this dreary matter of a division between
these Colonies & their benevolent Sovereign is soon brought to a
conclusion, the guilty dealt with summarily, the duped acquainted
with the error of their ways & set back to productive paths, & the
innocent permitted to return to felicitous peace. I continue to avidly
read all notices of the progress of the war in your parts, & to listen
for rumours of its impending conclusion. I hope to soon read of your
hand the happy details of that end, together with such expressions
of joy that they may yet reach my shriveled heart. Until I shall
again behold your cheerful thoughts, I am,*

      Your Sister,
      Susannah

On another cheerless excursion to the mercantile,
to ask after supplies that were no longer available at any
price, and much less to a girl whose father's accounts
were in arrears, Susannah fell into conversation with
Missus MacFarland, whose friendly and garrulous
nature penetrated even the gloom of Susan's mood.

Leaning against the counter at the till, she said,
"I have been at work in this store or one very like it for
three-and-twenty years, young Miss Susannah, and I
have never yet beheld such a visage of sadness as yours
is today."

Susannah replied, listlessly, "You know well
enough the causes, Missus MacFarland. What have I
to be happy for?"

The shopkeeper's wife smiled to herself for a
moment, and replied, "What, indeed. You are in the
bloom of your youth, you attract the eye of every
worthwhile boy about—and yes, a few unworthy, as
well—and if your current state is not so grand as you

had thought or hoped it would be, you have all the gifts to turn even a barrel of sour and reeking apples into a cider that makes all who behold it glad."

Susannah regarded the woman for a long moment, sighed, and said, "I wish that I could so clearly see what you do. At present, it is difficult to chart any path that leads from where I am to the kind of future I had intended for myself."

Missus MacFarland gave her a quizzical look and asked, crisply, "What sort of future is that?"

Susannah started to answer, and the shopkeeper's wife held up her hand quickly and said, "No, think on this question for a bit before you answer. What do you want of your future?"

Susannah looked startled, and then furrowed her brow for a few moments, before she began to answer again. "I should like to make a good match, first of all. I should like very much to have skills useful to my husband, beyond those which may be attended to by any serving-girl."

The shopkeeper's wife nodded. "'Tis a good start. How would you accomplish those things, had events gone as you had hoped?"

"My lessons with Master Grant should not have been interrupted when my father's business suffered certain reverses. As it is, I have continued to study both my primer and the books which Master Grant did lend me prior to his dismissal."

Missus MacFarland nodded again, with growing enthusiasm. "Have you attended your father when he works on his accounts and figures? There is much to learn in that exercise, I can assure you."

"I have not been so bold as to suggest such a thing."

"While he may not be eager to have you look on them when they are—as I surmise is the case—in disarray, and yet there is no time when it is more critical to know how to manage the accounts of an enterprise than when it is under some threat."

Briskly, she continued, "And what of correspondence? I know that you maintain a regular cycle of letters to and from your girlhood friend in Massachusetts Colony, which is admirable, particularly given the difficulty involved in the regular transmission of such letters, but have you studied at all the forms of commercial correspondence which might be of use to your future husband's enterprise?"

"Only slightly, in that Papa has at times shared with me the choicer bits of correspondence relating to uncomfortable transactions, but I have much to learn on that account, as well."

"And have you given any consideration to what sort of enterprise in which you should like for your future husband to be engaged? Do your interests lie outside or within your father's field of imports, or should you be satisfied to guide the affairs of a farmstead freehold?"

Susannah shook her head in grave negation. "I would rather not be engaged in such heavy work. Not—" she flushed, then continued, "Not that I am opposed to manual work; when called for by circumstance, 'tis noble indeed. However, I flatter myself to think that I am capable of more valuable occupations to my spouse."

Missus MacFarland pursed her lips, but nodded thoughtfully. "Be not shy about taking on the hard work of the hands and back, when they are called for, but also be not shy about assessing your value, as you have done. Are you satisfied that there are ways to move toward your goals, even without the ideal scenes you had imagined coming to pass?"

Susannah scowled for a moment, and then said reluctantly, "Indeed have you shown me that not all is as dark as I thought it when I arrived here."

The woman smiled broadly at Susannah, and then said, "I shall make you a solemn vow. If, one year hence, to the day, you can walk in this door and tell me that you are truly no happier on that day than you are now, I shall hand you over ten pounds sterling, to do with as you wish."

Susannah gaped at the woman. This was a stupendous sum of money to be wagering so blithely. "I shall return on that date, to report truthfully whether I am then lower than I am today." She had a mischievous thought, and continued, "I cannot but think, though, that you shall have the better of this wager, because the knowledge of gaining such riches will bring me joy, which would stop me from collecting, resulting in my being lower yet."

She grinned at the shopkeeper's wife and said, accusingly, "'Tis a trick, I now see, but it has already worked its magic, and I feel less unhappy than when I came in here."

"You see? There is always something to be happy for." She leaned in closer to the girl and said, in a more conspiratory tone, "Now, should you like some news of the town to further distract your mind from your own worries?"

Susannah leaned in, herself, and nodded. Missus MacFarland fulfilled many roles in the community, but the disseminator of news of the town was probably the most valuable service she provided, and that she did just for the joy of it.

"Your old friend Colin, as well as many others

of the valley, have been lately involved in rebellious activities."

Susannah gasped, and the a sage expression asserted itself on the woman's broad face. "'Tis said that they continue to plot with the rioters who were defeated at Cumberland. The Marines may have to go back in to put them down, and 'tis anyone's guess as to whether it will be resolved through words or bloodshed."

She looked thoughtful, and added, "They have long grievances, and it is not easy to set those aside, even in the face of a superior force of arms, when you believe that you have the right of the argument."

Looking back at Susannah, she said, "Another rumor I have heard about these parts is that it may come to skirmish between them and the newly-settled Yorkshiremen, as those worthies have good reason to be grateful to the Crown, and those of rebellious sentiment are not inclined to be humble before them, feeling that the newcomers have been given more than they deserved, particularly with our supplies being so sorely pressed in these days."

Susannah's lips compressed into a tight expression of concern, and she said, "Colin and his intended lie on opposing sides of that gap, and he has been dependent upon her father for his livelihood. Has he placed his imagined political grievances above the value of his heart?"

Missus MacFarland said, "I know aught of such details, but it stands to reason that he may have placed that relationship in some jeopardy by throwing his lot in with the rioters."

Susannah, her expression reflecting both concern and consideration of the possibilities, nodded, and then said, "I should be going, as Papa will be wondering whether I have got lost along the way. I will relate to him the sad fact that those items for which I came hither are not to be had on this day, either, and shall convey your greetings to him."

The shopkeeper's wife nodded a slow, wise farewell and continued to smile after the girl, long after the door had banged shut behind her.

Chapter 17

March the Seventh, Seventeen Seventy-Seven

My Dear Sister Susannah,
Though as I write it, the date seems as though it ought to be Auspicious, the notices we here receive of the progress of this long war against the rebellious Dogs of these Colonies are anything but. You will have been apprised by now of the events at New-Jersey, where our men and their Hessian allies were put on the run as the result of a Stroke of luck in favour of the rebels. Attacking during a snowstorm and whilst the noble Defenders are observing a solemn Holiday—what barbarian does such a Thing? We hear, too, that the Cabal controlling these Rebels has been emboldened enough to have returned to its former Seat in the wretched City of Philadelphia. They fly like cowardly Curs before the upright appearance of the King's Men, and when our forces must Retire the Field for a moment, they are as impudent Crows returned to cackle and taunt from the heights of their Safety. Oh, how I hope to hear soon of their Fall! Of course, I voice these Opinions frankly to you, and in the Privacy of my thoughts, but there is no Action that I may take in support of the King or of those bitter Few who here still cherish his Dominion over these Lands and their scattered Peoples. All that we who yet honour our Sovereign can do is to keep the Spark of respect for Obligation, for Tradition and for Service alive in our breasts.

I have received no Word from you in these many months since I last wrote to you—I trust that all is well in your Life? Has Mister Black's suit for your Heart so far progressed that you no longer have Time to write to your devoted Sister, I wonder? I suppose that Time will reveal all, but I am not a Patient girl, as you know well. Of my own Callers, I can say with an Honest and Direct voice that only one or two have so much as turned my Head. One such is Mister Jonah Allen, whom you may slightly Remember, as the half-lamed eldest Son of five to our Friend and Neighbour, his Father, the Chaplain, who has removed himself to England to avoid our current National Convulsions. Jonah chose to remain here and to Pursue the career in the manufacture of Soap, which seems both most Charming and Lucrative to me, for all Men, regardless of their Affiliations, have need of Soap, if only to satisfy the Demands of their Wives' desire for Cleanliness. He has learnt his craft at apprenticeship to one Nathaniel Jakes, who has since then gone on from this Country to another. The Details of his work are quite a Mystery to me, tho he does try to convey to my mind the Measurements of the various Components of his Wares, and from whence he procures these Ingredients, a task which is, by his Account, quite complicated by the interruptions to trade. Suffice to say that it is an Intricate pursuit, and one which most Satisfies his mind. On the other hand, there is Mister Richard Hazzard, whose Occupation is not at all clear to those who Observe him, even as closely as I do. He has a great deal of Interaction with men of Means in this area, however, and seems at all Times to be more than merely Prosperous. I am fair certain that he is no Smuggler, as he evinces no particular Knowledge of the sea, nor of the Movement of Goods, and is,

*indeed, full ignorant of the ruinous Prices of so many Things
in these troubled days. Last week, I was working a bit of clever
Embroidery when he called, and broke a needle, which caused
me to let fly a most vext and ill-considered Curse in his gentle
presence. By way of Explanation, I gave him to understand
that needles were difficult to replace, and dear to the Purse, he
expressed outright Amazement that so small an item should do
so much harm to one's Wallet. May I tell you frankly that it was
wondrous Charming to be so unguarded with a Gentleman for
once? I do not think that he is liable to press his Suit for me,
as I am of too modest Means to make a good Match to him,
but it is pleasant to pass an Afternoon with a person who is,
at turns, marvelously Knowledgeable and splendidly Naïve.
Outside of these relatively petty Distractions, life continues here
much as it has since the Tumult of active Rebellion passed from
these lands to other Colonies. There are, on Occasion, upsets,
as when a man in the town next over was accused of Spying
for the King, and was placed upon the Gallows, with his neck
in a Noose, and lash'd until he had confessed to all manner of
unlikely and strange Sins against his neighbours, his family and
God Himself, few of which could be corroborated by any other
evidence, but which were as a body enough for him to gain his
Release. Indeed, it seems as though his greatest sin was in the
Imagination that it required to invent such tales to satisfy his
Tormentors. Eventually, they tired of so Abusing him, and he
regained his Freedom, as well as the attention of every Gossip
all the country round. I'll not here rehearse his stories, but to say
that they were as lurid as they were improbable, and counter
to all Sense and Propriety. I will leave you, my Sister, with a
pleasant thought—regardless the outcome of this Contest of wills*

between the King and his former Subjects in these Colonies, we shall in later years be entertained by the many such Stories from these days which we may relate. 'Tis but a small comfort, in truth, but we must find our comforts where we may among the Grim Days of war. Awaiting your next missive with eagerness, I am,

    Your Devoted Sister,
    Emma

Susannah set the letter aside and shook her head. Such dizzying days these were, indeed. On her visit earlier that day to the mercantile, where the letter awaited her, she had learned of a series of events that seemed still to be the creation of some fabulist, and not the result of actual events affecting people whom she thought she had known.

After she had picked up a small packet of coarse flour, and received her letter from the Mister MacFarland, she had left the shop to find that a large crowd milled about the front stoop, surrounding a soldier, whom they were interrogating eagerly. The soldier's face shone with pride and joy, and as she approached, Susannah could hear the happy man telling his tale.

"'Twere a fearsome force there gathered, comprising some hundreds of rebels in their numbers, augmented in their positions by leaders aboard their boat from Machais. Bold as brass, they was, and full of rude jeers, though they were soon enough cured of that when we hove to."

He paused to pull a kerchief from his pocket and wipe down his brow. Storytelling was, it seemed, a thirsty and tiring task. "Them rabble-rousers from Maine took off to running into the forest when they beheld us at the entrance to the harbor, and it was without any particular difficulty that we took their boat, and two others besides, laden with all manner of cargo. Some of it were practical stuff, but some were oddities, said to belong to some trader in these parts, and taken by fraud."

He shrugged, as Susannah's blood ran cold and she caught her breath, almost missing what the soldier added next. "We captured with his boat the defaulter who had committed that theft and delivered him to the appropriate authorities here, upon our return. In the event, though we would have liked to have pursued those villains from Maine into the forest, they had clearly acquainted themselves with the territory, and had help from the people of the town, as well."

He nodded with smug satisfaction and went on, "But we gave them townspeople a fair what-for, I can tell you that. We stood to, unable to come ashore yet in safety, but with our guns trained upon the town. 'Taint much that will stand before a barrage such as we were prepared to delivered, and all and sundry about knew it well."

His smile widened even further as someone in the crowd handed him a fresh mug of cider, and he warmed to his tale. "The Colonel, he sent ashore a man under a flag of truce, and delivered a notice to the rebels of the town that they could be paroled and would be suffered even to retain their homes and property, if they would but sign a fresh oath of allegiance to the Crown. 'Twere more generous than many of us were prepared to treat them to, but as they had given us no fight after their traitorous leaders abandoned them, it were well-taken to offer them quarter."

He nodded and took a long drink. "Of course,

though they had been led astray, them people in the town knew that they had no hope of prevailing, and that they had the lesser of the fight, if it came to that. So they sent a boat forth in two days' time, agreeing to all terms without reservation, and that were the end of the engagement, save for returning the seized ships hither. 'Tis said that the government is seeking for the rightful owner of the one ship, and so if any here know who that might be, you might do him a service and send him down to the customs-house."

Susannah did not say anything, but hurriedly made her way through the crowd, and fairly sprinted for home. If it were true, if Providence had chosen to smile upon her father, after so sorely testing him, all of the despair of the days past might be lifted. She remembered Roger as she ran, and corrected herself— nearly all despair.

Chapter 18

May the Twelfth, anno domini 1777

My Dear Sister Emma,

I know not whether you have received my last letter, or whether it was misdirected on its perilous way to you; setting that aside, however, all is changed now, though not all to the better. My father has lost a partner, & I a suitor, to the shifting chances of war; that much is now certain. In the fortnight past, my father's fortunes were restored by the return of a ship, thought taken by the rebels, but in fact delivered unto them willingly by that accursed Roger Black, a secret sympathiser with their disloyal cause. By his perfidy, we were to be ruined, & this ruination considered as the just results of war. In the event, though, his treason was discovered during the prosecution of an attack on the town nearby here of Saint John, which had been spurred to rebellion by agents of the disloyal Colonies. The King's Men went forth to there, seeking to put down their ill-considered movement, & discovered three ships lying at anchor, one of which was filled up with goods purchased on Papa's good credit. With that ship restored to his control, he was able to both provide some little creature comfort to the long-deprived people of this town & the places nearby, but he has been returned to a goodly prosperity, which is a most welcome event. I tell you truly that money is not necessary to happiness, *but it certainly gives a more likely prospect to the pursuit thereof. Alas, but my happiness is somewhat disrupted by the untrue heart which pretended to pursue mine, with a single bold kiss (but do not tell Papa), & a considered pattern of flirtation, pretty compliments & small gifts. Beware the dressed-up speech of those who seek something of you with the one hand, even as they offer you false promises of the heart with the other! I am fortunate to have had Mister Black's discourteous lies revealed to me before I gave him any real ground in the pursuit of his designs upon my heart, but I will not pretend to have escaped unwounded. I will not be so easily won over by any other man's flattery, I assure you most fervently. A man whose disloyalty to King & Country is so deeply concealed may not be trusted ever to be capable of true loyalty to his helpmeet & friends. So much for Mister Black; his fate lies now in the hands of the Admiralty Court, as he stands now accused of outright piracy on the high seas, & they are not inclined toward clemency, nor toward a lengthy process of justice. I should be surprised indeed if he fails to dance upon the hangman's noose before another fortnight is past. I shall not grieve further, should that come to pass; I have grieved already for the loss of the man I thought I knew, so why should I waste any tears in grief for the man he turned out to be? Of the two suitors of whom you write, I am inclined to favour Mister Allen, whose honest trade & straightforward pursuit of you are both more worthy & more likely to ensure future happiness than Mister Hazzard, whose very name, not to mention his mysterious manner of earning his bread, both give one reason to pause & consider whether any part of his story may truly be trusted. I know that you did not seek my advice with your letter, but I shall offer it none-the-less, having so recently learnt a hard lesson in these matters myself. Better that you learn by my error than that only I shall attempt to take its lessons to heart. I am sorry to hear that the war within our nation fares no more clearly than that within our respective hearts. Is all to be endless conflict, forever & ever without relief? I know not, & I fear to learn the truth in the weeks & months that lie before us. Woe be to us, born to such a time of strife! I wish that I had some happier note on which to end this letter, but outside of the minor matter of the return of my father's prosperity & the coming of the kinder season of Spring in these parts, there seems precious little true happiness to share at this time. I hope that you have more joyful news to report when I next behold a letter from you. Until that time, I remain,*

   Your Faithful & Loving Sister,
   Susannah

Missus MacFarland was glad to see her when Susannah arrived at the mercantile, carrying the letter for dispatch, and a list of small things that her step-mother had requested that she seek for there.

"Ah, 'tis my favorite fortune-turner," she exclaimed as Susannah handed over her letter and the coins to pay its passage to New England.

Susannah smiled and shook her head ruefully. "I shall not live that down, shall I?"

"Never in my life, my dear child. I must say that Mister MacFarland is glad for it, too, as himself was quite concerned that I was going to have to yield up the ten pounds I'd wagered." She laughed lightly as she glanced fondly back at the residence portion of the structure.

The door swung open, and a familiar figure stepped through. Susannah felt her face go hot in recollection of the last time she had seen Colin here, and the shopkeeper's wife's expression turned immediately sympathetically serious.

She called out to him, "What brings you all the way into town today, Master McRae?"

Walking up to the till, he nodded gravely to Susannah, and then turned to Missus MacFarland, and spoke quietly. "My Pa sends me to fetch back some tea and a small bottle of sack, if you should have it."

She pursed her lips and replied, "Tea I have, but no sack has arrived to these shores in some months, Colin. I'll keep you in mind, though, should I secure any supplies of the like."

He nodded gratefully as she turned away and busied herself with the tea. She asked over her shoulder, "How much did he want?"

"Just four ounces, if I may," he answered, his voice still quiet. He turned to face Susannah, took a deep breath, and asked, "How are you today, Miss Mills?"

She replied, as evenly as she could with her heart racing in spite of herself, "Tolerably well, Master McRae." Determined to not steer clear of the unseen issue in the room between them, she asked, "What news is there of your impending nuptials?"

He blushed furiously and his eyes narrowed as he looked away from her. Clearly, he would have been happier had the issue remained unspoken. "Miss Stayton and I are no longer in any form of communication, owing to my recent misadventures."

Susannah feigned shock, but then said with genuine puzzlement, "I am sincerely sorry to hear that, but I am not acquainted with any misadventures of yours—of what do you speak?"

Susannah noticed that Missus MacFarland finished wrapping the tea and set it aside, and then made herself busy at the furthest possible end of the counter. Colin pressed his hands to his forehead and squeezed, as if to push a bad memory right out of his mind. "You know that I had become enamored of some of what the rebels in these parts had been saying."

Her mouth firmed into a thin line, and she nodded.

He dropped his hands and looked her straight in the eye. "I have learned the error of my ways, but it has cost me dear." He took another deep breath, and repeated, "It has cost me dear."

Her mouth softened somewhat, but she said, "I confess that I have a hard time feeling much sympathy for your reverses when they have resulted from disloyalty to your King and Country."

He nodded, and said, "I understand why you feel that way, and believe me, I harbor no disloyal thought in my mind any longer."

She pondered for a moment and then motioned with her hand for him to go on.

"I found myself in the village of Saint John this past winter, and when the men from Maine came through, having just besieged the fort at Cumberland, and having lived to tell the tale, well, it certainly got the attention of a number of us who had leaned in the direction of favoring a break from the King."

He got a distant, sad look in his eyes and was silent for a moment, but then picked up the thread of his story. "It was easy enough to get caught up in the thrill of the thing—you have good men on either side of you, and you're working together to make a better world, a brighter future, and you lose track of how good you world already is, how bright the present is."

His eyes brightened with unshed tears, but he ignored them, continuing, "When the Marines sailed in this past fortnight, we were ready to face them, even though we could see that our chances were slim. We knew that the men who led us were brave and pure of heart, and would stand with us to the very end, come what may."

He laughed bitterly and said, "They fled at their first chance, and left us all to twist in the wind in their stead. So much for principle, so much for freedom, so much for unity. The only thing that they cared about in the end was their own precious skins, and as far as they were concerned, we could all hang for their crimes."

He shrugged. "I have had ample opportunity to think about what decisions I made. I thought that the rebels were after building a world where no man needed to bow to another, and I discovered that when the moment for standing together arrived, we were expected to bow down on the behalf of those who considered themselves our betters.

"I believed that they sought to build a world where all would be free to practice their trade without interference, and I learned that such freedom was not meant for those whom they would have languish in a prison whilst they themselves wandered the country, raising more trouble."

He shook his head angrily. "I was convinced that I was participating in a new glorious revolution, and instead I found myself facing a shameful defeat, whilst those who were supposed to be our equals found themselves a new set of fools to deceive."

His chin sank to his chest as he continued, "I found only betrayal at the traitors' hands, and when our supposed tormentors appeared, and by all rights could have subjected us to a justice of the most eternal nature, they stayed their hands, and offered us mercy, indeed, redemption.

"They could have fired on the town, and destroyed us all, traitors and innocents alike. Instead, they offered us parole and leave to return to our homes and trades."

Susannah nodded slowly, saying softly, "I had heard of their mercy toward the rebellious forces. I did not know then that their mercy would spare a friend his life."

He chewed his lower lip, as though trying to stay tears that threatened to overcome him, before he continued, "Mister Stayton—Michelle's father—had made for me a home on his farmstead; I returned to find that it was already leased out to a family who shared his views, and my few belongings were rotting in the mud at the back step. He will not let me so much as see Michelle, though he did suffer her to send me a letter laying out my many failings as a human being."

He shook his head ruefully. "She had much to say that was simply untrue, and much that was wide of the mark. Since she so rarely spoke her mind, she had developed an entire theory of my person against which I never had any opportunity of defense."

He straightened his shoulders and looked Susannah in the eye steadily. "She did say one thing in her letter, though, which hit the mark squarely. She said that she could never marry a man who pined so deeply for another, and that she could never marry a man who was already in love when she found him."

Susannah took a moment to put the words he had spoken together, and then her eyes narrowed, and she demanded, "Michelle thought that you loved me?"

"Michelle is quiet, but she sees all, and she probably knows both of us better even than we know ourselves. She also said that she believed that I was not the only one who pined, and that her only consolation was that you are too loyal to the King, and too proud to ever consider relieving my sad existence without her."

Susannah regarded Colin with an inscrutable expression for such a long time that neither one of them was certain what words she might utter next. Finally, she said quietly, "Your tea is ready," and turned and left.

Chapter 19

June the 23rd, Seventeen Seventy-Seven

My Sister Susannah,
Such terrible days have we here had these past months!
Not long after I dispatched my last letter to you, my Father
came under suspicion of providing Aid of some variety to the
King's Men in far-off New-York. While none can yet provide
any Answer for what caused the foul Rebels to put to him to
the Test, I can assure you that he never took any untoward
Action against the violent and dangerous Bullies who form
what we may laughingly refer to as the Authorities in these
parts. Without any Warrant or advance Warning of any sort, a
group of Men came to our door in the night and seized my Dear
Father, treating him with exceptional Roughness as they so did.
They refused all entreaties for Explanation, and drove away
with him Cruelly Bound and Hooded, leaving my Mother and
I Defenceless and in a state of utter Terror for three whole
days, the like of which I never hope to Endure again. At the
end of that time, with no more Explanation than when our
trial Began, my beloved Father was returned to us, ill-treated
and much damaged with Bruises and other Marks of Abuse.
Mother has nursed him back to Health, tending to his wounds,
but he has so far steadfastly Refused all efforts to prise from him
any Account of his experience whilst in the Grip of our Terror.

This Incident has proven to be a matter of no small Effect upon his Character, as he is no longer able to Stand upright without severe pain, nor will he Speak with real Feeling in any matter that once aroused his Passions. I have overheard the piteous Discussions between him and Mother, and I have from these learnt that he is Consumed with Regret for not removing our family from these Rebel Parts when the way was open to do so. Having fallen under the Suspicion of our Cruel new Masters, we are no longer afforded any Freedom to depart, nor are we made Welcome to stay. We exist in a grey Purgatory while we wait for the Contest of Arms to elsewhere be settled. The only Good to have come of this wretched Affair is that my friend Jonas Allen has been a great Comfort to us all, and has taken up the Duties of a Son, even before he has sought the Privileges of a Suitor. My heart is much warmed by his Friendship, and I confess that I am eager for him to Declare his suit for me at the earliest Date possible. You are correct, of course, about the suspicious nature of the man who I once thought might be a Rival to Mister Allen. Tho I have not told him in so many Words that I will no longer entertain any Question from him, he has quite disappeared from our Home, now that it has cast over it a Shadow of suspicion. Increasing the Mystery of our Suffering is the fact that there remains no Action in these parts to which one could Attach any military significance. There is no open Challenge to the Insurrection, and our Conduct as a household has ever been Exemplary. Even when told that we must Yield up taxes to support the Maintenance of those Troops from the town who carry arms in Opposition to the King, we have made no Protest, and have paid what is Demanded of us. We are, all of us, in a state of Confusion and Fear, a condition

which we all anticipate will be some time in waiting for Relief.
Your Letters are a Support to me, and I await your next with
no small Anticipation. Until then, I remain,
        Your Sister,
        Emma

Fear, Susannah reflected as she brought in water for the day from the well behind the new house, seemed to be the watchword of this era. While she felt relatively secure in her person here in Halifax, everywhere else in the province seemed to be under the constant threat of American raiders sweeping in from the sea and taking what they liked, as if they were the Danes of old.

Farmsteads, whose situation near to the sea had once seemed a blessing, were now being abandoned, as there was little point in raising a crop for the benefit of thieves and pirates. The town of Saint John, which had so recently been a friendly haven for the rebels, had been raided so often that there were calls to station a garrison there to protect the King's subjects, newly sworn to loyalty, and suffering for it.

Colin's father had not yet been forced to leave his farmstead, although Colin himself was a more frequent fixture in town of late. He had not pressed Susannah for any answer to the declaration of his feelings, but had simply remained... present. She frowned as she reached the door and set down the water bucket to lift the latch. She still could not decide whether she could find it in herself to trust her heart to his sincerity.

She was glad, however, to have restored even some part of their ruptured friendship. She enjoyed encountering him at the mercantile, and they not infrequently turned out to be going in the same direction when they met on the street. He was no less interesting to talk with than before their break, and he was a sympathetic ear when she needed one badly.

Roger Black had been in due course found guilty of treason, but instead of the hanging that she expected to endure, he had, through the inexplicable intercession of her father, been sentenced instead to transportation over the sea back to England, where he would be imprisoned for a term of years, and then released there—but barred from ever returning to the King's Colonies in America.

Susannah had not understood her father's motivation for arguing for clemency for Black, and on a stroll with Colin, she had spoken to him quite vehemently of it. "This traitor took advantage of Papa's trust, and used his good name to the advantage and very nearly to the substantial material benefit of the Rebel cause. And yet he is given the benefit of my father's testimony on his behalf? It beggars understanding!"

Colin, as was his habit, gave the question some thought before answering. "It may be that there are some qualities to Mister Black's character with which you are less acquainted than is your father, as his erstwhile business partner."

She flushed slightly, and then answered, "It is true that the primary qualities of Mister Black's character with which I am familiar are those which accompany his attempt to deceive the heart of a woman." Colin looked at her sharply, but she chose to ignore the unstated question of his glance. "I heard much at the time from Papa, however, of his efforts on behalf of their intended business, and it seems in retrospect that many of those were primarily related to his glibness in making deals with the suppliers."

She shook her head in quick negation. "Those

same suppliers were as deceived as was Papa, and the damage resulting from his lies threatened to put many of them out of business entirely. It was only through a stroke of good fortune that all was restored to its rightful order, as you know. Without that, our entire family would have been plunged into even further poverty, and many other good men would have suffered ruin or substantial reverses, as well."

Colin said nothing, but continued to walk beside Susannah, apparently examining the ground before them closely.

She pursed her lips in silent frustration, until a new thought struck her. "Is it possible that Mister Black gained some secret intelligence about Papa that he might have threatened to reveal, without Papa should agree to assist in his case?"

Colin scoffed, "Would he not have taken that intelligence to the gallows with him, had his case gone as anticipated?"

Susannah frowned. "I cannot counter your logic," she conceded.

"Have you simply asked your father directly?"

Susannah huffed in irritation and answered, "No, for I am not sure that he even knows the reason for his action."

Colin glanced over at her with a sly smile. "He might surprise you, you know. We men do sometimes know the workings of our own mind, often nearly as much as do the women who know us."

Susannah rolled her eyes at him, and walked on beside him, silent in her turn.

They arrived at the house—not quite as grand as the first she and her father had engaged upon their arrival, but easily the nicest that was available after his fortunes had reverted to the side of success—and she turned to Colin formally. "Thank you for your company, Mister McRae. I shall anticipate our next conversation with pleasure."

He returned her formality, giving her a stiff little bow and saying, "The pleasure of this walk is all mine, and I likewise look forward to our next encounter. Good day to you, Miss Mills." He turned and walked away, tossing a small, sardonic smile over his shoulder as he went.

It was a little game between them that he had initiated the first time that they had walked together after his confession about the note from Michelle. Susannah had appreciated the opportunity to set aside the awkward question of whether or not they might be courting by substituting the formality of this farewell for the forms of courtship.

She opened the front door and called out, "I am home, Papa," as she entered. She saw him wave from the study, and went in to join him. Perhaps there was something to Colin's suggestion, though she wasn't sure how to begin.

She decided to simply inquire as directly as possible. "Papa, I have been giving the matter substantial thought, and I cannot make sense of your decision to defend Mister Black's life on the dock. Should not the law have been permitted to take its course, and to have pronounced the expected sentence upon his life?"

Her father closed the account-book he had been examining and pushed back from his desk with a long, thoughtful sigh. "I am surprised only that you have not asked me this sooner, Susannah. I know that you felt extremely the betrayal of our business, as well as no small amount of betrayal of your heart."

Susannah blushed and he smiled gently. "Oh, yes, I was aware that he had begun to pursue you, though he never made bold enough to ask my permission to court you. He has enough honesty in him that I think that would have been a deception too grave for even his false heart to have carried off."

Susannah frowned, but he continued, "The fact of the matter is that while I could have borne his death for the acts that brought harm to this family, his crimes were not against us, but against the King. The courts take some notice, though, of victims outside of the Crown, and your mother and I discussed this question at great length."

He smiled gaily and said, "As you might imagine, she is no bloodthirsty being, unlike me, and, I think, unlike you. We are willing enough to see blood spilled when the occasion calls for it, but she is a gentler being, and talked me into acting as I could to ensure that Mister Black's life was spared, but that he suffered sufficiently for his crimes."

Nodding to himself, he said, "Think of it, Susannah. He will now languish in a prison in England, alongside men who, though they be criminals, are still loyal to the King. Once his sentence is served, he is not permitted the courtesy of leaving England, but must instead live out the rest of his days among the people whose interests in America he acted to destroy."

He looked at Susannah with an expression of grim satisfaction, and concluded, "I believe that Mister Roger Black was given a sentence far more severe than the release of death. He is, rather, sentenced to life with the knowledge of his treason spread far and wide. No honest man will ever treat with him again, and he knows no other trade. I am well enough satisfied with his punishment, and I think if you give it sufficient consideration, you will be, too."

Chapter 20

September the Fifth,
anno domini Seventeen Seventy-Seven

My Dear Sister Emma,

Our trials here continue, though we are assured of some improvement with the establishment of a new blockhouse at Saint John, dispatched from this town in the fortnight past. To be called Fort Howe, honouring that selfsame brave General Howe who has, by all accounts, been giving the rebel Washington all manner of trouble in New-York & Pennsylvania. Oh, how I pray on each passing day that we shall receive a dispatch announcing that the rebel's main army has suffered its inevitable total defeat, & that our forces stand victorious over them. The temporary setbacks suffered by our men early in this year seem to have been exceptions, & the overall tide of the war continues to augur well for our success, though we must remain both patient & vigilant for that happy day. In the mean time, I have again been keeping company with Mister Colin McRae, whose engagement with our former serving-girl was broken off on account of his foolhardy dalliance in support of the rebels. He has learned a hard lesson thereby, & has sworn a fresh & binding oath of allegiance to the King & his duly appointed representatives in these Colonies. In the course of this, he has had the opportunity to examine his heart most closely, & he *has made several discoveries—some of which were even suggested by his former intended. Most importantly, he learned that he was in love with your faithful correspondent, a discovery which I consider as unwelcome as it was unforeseen. I have valued him as a friend & a confidant, but I had not considered him as a suitor in any sense at all. Between the sudden change in the loyalty of his political interests & that of his heart, let us just say that I am treading very, very lightly & with great caution & deliberation. It is a pleasure, though, to pass time with him, & he is a most energetic & animated conversationalist. I know not what future lies before us, but if it is meant to be courtship, then I will accept that without complaint. It hardly seems possible that it has been three full years since we arrived at these shores, & very nearly that long since first I met Colin. While our first meeting may have been inauspicious—mud, tears, & an ankle that swelled to the size of my knee!—he has shown me naught but kindness, even as we suffered a falling out over political disagreements. His swift engagement thereafter was an error, & one which I have not permitted him to repeat by taking up any pursuit of my hand in the immediacy of his new loss. I do hope that this letter finds you well, & your situation both clarified & settled. Until I shall again see your sentiments, I remain,*

> *Your Loving Sister,*
> *Susannah*

Donning her old bearskin coat against an unseasonably cold day, Susannah strolled along the road that fronted the docks, taking in the sights and sounds there. Alongside her, Colin walked, his hands shoved resolutely within his own coat. He was looking somewhat downcast, as she'd declined to take his arm as they walked.

"It looks overly familiar, Colin," she said in exasperation. "I do not deny that the day may come when it is appropriate that you offer your arm, but that I have not yet consented that you ask my father for that privilege."

He'd said nothing, his face taking on a stubborn expression as he walked. Gangs of teamsters, their sleeves shoved back over their arms despite the cold, labored to load up wagons from a newly-arrived ship. Goods from England herself, it looked like, bound for destinations throughout the region. Susannah made a mental note to stop in at the mercantile later, to check on the availability of a few herbs unobtainable here, but which her step-mother was always hoping to secure.

Finally, Colin spoke, quietly, but firmly. "I know that I gave you great offense by my actions, both in my foolhardy involvement with the rebels, and in my ill-conceived attachment to Michelle. However, I feel more certain in this than I have any other thing in my life: I must learn whether we are meant to be together."

He stopped and faced her, his expression earnest. "Out of respect for your well-deserved outrage at my actions, I have kept my counsel to this point, and I have not pressed you for any answer to my interest. It is enough for me, most days, to simply know that we are friends."

Susannah interrupted to ask, "Then cannot we remain simply friends for some decent time after your broken engagement, that both we and those who observe us closely may be certain that you are not committing the error of seeking solace in the arms of any convenient companion who will have you?"

He stammered, "I—I hadn't considered it in that light. I thought only that you sought to punish me for my errors and faults."

She tilted her head at him, smiling. "It is not yet my place to punish you for what errors you may make. Should that day arrive, you may trust that I will discharge those duties of friendship with all proper diligence."

In spite of himself, Colin laughed. "'Tis likely to be a fulsome occupation, given my tendency to err and your strength at detecting and giving voice to those errors as you perceive them."

She laughed with him, and they returned to strolling along together. They made the turn up to her father's home, and parted at the door with a wave. Their conversation for the rest of their walk concerned lighter, less consequential matters, such as the rumors of sightings of American raiders along the shore south of town, and speculation as to the effective range of the guns of the newly-completed fort that overlooked the harbor.

As she stepped inside and closed the door behind her, Susannah felt a sense of relief that they had finally discussed and understood one another over the issue of his proposed pursuit of her. She was not entertaining any other callers, but she did feel strongly that his motivations needed to be completely clear to himself, and to those in the village who might stand in judgment of his actions.

The next morning, she went down to the mercantile as she had planned, after asking her step-mother what specific items might be of best utility to her at this time. The day was bright and cold, and what leaves still stood upon the trees at the edges of town were starting to lose the bright hues of autumn. She entered the shop to a cheerful greeting from Missus MacFarland.

"Good morning, my dear Miss Susannah. Before I forget, I have a letter here for you. But what do you come here after this bright day?"

Susannah walked up to the counter and leaned against it happily. "Mother has sent me hither with a short list of items which she had hoped might have come in on the recent ship from England." She offered the shopkeeper's wife the list, and accepted the letter that the woman held out in exchange. She glanced at the cover and her brow furrowed. "'Tis a shame that our correspondence crossed in transit."

Missus McRae looked up from the list and nodded. "Indeed. Odd thing, too—this one came in with the ship from England, and not on the normal packet up from General Howe's stronghold." She returned to scanning the list. "I think we did take delivery of a couple of these items, yes. Let me go fetch them up for you."

Susannah broke open the seal on the letter while she waited and began to read. At the first lines, her eyes widened, and by the time she had rushed through the letter to its end, she had her hand up to her mouth in shock.

Chapter 21

July 25th, 1777

My Dear Sister,
    So much has come to pass so Swiftly that I scarcely know where to begin. After I dispatched my latest letter to you, my dear Father, who had never really Recovered himself following his cruel Abuse at the hands of the Vicious rebels, declined swiftly into a Crisis, the finality of which was plain to see. As it became apparent to all that his End was fast approaching, Mister Allen immediately proposed Marriage, which I accepted with what Joy I could gather under the grim Circumstance that spurred it. We were wed before the week was out, whilst my Dear, Devoted Father could yet consent and witness, and then we buried my Father the Sunday following, ultimately broken and Humiliated by the wicked Rebel Mob. My husband and I spoke at length with my black-garbed Mother, and we prevailed upon her to remove to England by the first available means. And so I write to you from the noisome town of Portsmouth, in the south of England herself. How curious and Strange are the people here, to one who was born in the Colonies and has only ever known the ways of Home! They have neither Patience nor any particular Sympathy for our Situation, which, tho 'tis not dire in particular, leaves also much to be desired. Jonas has already established contact with a man who is eager for a

skilled assistant in the soapmaking Business. As my husband excels at his Trade, we shall not be long in establishing an independent Shop for him, a point upon which Jonas has been at Pains to clarify with his potential Employer here, lest there be any Misunderstanding later. We have secured here a tidy little Home, with space enough for Jonas and I and my Mother, who is Bearing Up as well as may be Expected. We are all still Shocked by the turn of Events that has Whisked us hither, against all Expectation. I am filled with Despair, as well, at the sad Thought that you and I are now Separated not only by a hostile Frontier, but by a great Ocean, the crossing of which is no small Feat, and one that I shall hope not to Repeat under such dire Conditions again. But—you know a bit about Travel over Seas while your heart is in Tatters. I am in constant Vacillation between Joy at having made such an Auspicious Marriage, as well as having Removed to a place far from the Tumult of War, and complete Collapse in Sadness at all that passed before these Happy Turns. There is, as well, the Confusion which will naturally attend a sudden Translation to a Foreign Land, for tho this Place ought to be as familiar as our Mother is to us, its Customs are entirely more Formal and Rigid than I like, and its people less Forgiving of unintended Trespasses against these Customs. 'Tis a minor Hardship amongst all the Others which I have hitherto Endured, but it Contributes greatly to my Unease in my new Home. I confess that upon our arrival, I did behold a most curious Sight, which gave me further Cause to wonder about the true Safety we might here enjoy. Above the entrance to the Harbour of this town there stands upon the Gibbet a most piteous set of remains, being the last mortal pieces of a most heinous Criminal, lately caught in these parts. He was known as Jack the Painter, and upon declaring his attachment to the Violent Cause of Rebellion in America that we have just escaped, he did undertake to commit Acts of destruction upon these shores. He succeeded only in firing the rope-house at the Royal Navy's great Shipyards here, but even that caused a great Disruption and Upset in these parts. It comes as small Comfort to my distressed Mind that he was captured in due course, and brought to a Swift and certain End, his corpse left to Dangle here as a visible Warning to all who might Conceive of a misplaced Notion to follow his example. So even at this Remove, in a strange land across Seas, I cannot be wholly Assured of the safety which we here sought. I must Persevere, however, as this Change is one that I will in later years much Value for all the positive Results it shall have wrought. I desire to get this letter onto the Ship which I have learnt is bound for your Port this very day, so I must here end it, so as to deliver it to the Purser thereon. You may direct your replies to me care of the The Bell Tavern here in Portsmouth, which Establishment lies quite close by our new home. I remain, however separated by the Miles,

> *Your Devoted Sister,*
> *Emma*

Susannah walked home from the mercantile, barely aware of the parcel that Missus MacFarland had thrust into her hands after hearing the outline of the news carried in the letter. She recalled Emma's father, a hardworking, jovial man, a bit liberal with the port wine after a meal, but always quick to pass along a kind word when a young friend of his daughter needed it.

The thought that he should have ended his days

in decline as a result of having been ill-used by rioting Whiggish monsters made her blood boil, and it was a matter of good fortune that Colin did not appear, as was his wont, to accompany her on her walk home, for she did not feel that she could have resisted the urge to heap abuse upon him for ever having willingly associated himself with their cause.

And, almost more startling, Emma, a full year and a half her junior, should be married away, and a wife, with so little warning. Susannah had a thousand questions about her friend's new husband, most of which would have been better asked and answered prior to the commitment being made. Now that they were joined, all that she could do was to pray that they had not acted rashly.

Her mind strayed to an older friend of theirs, Diane, who had been hurried into an ill-conceived marriage by certain scandalous circumstances. Their playful and happy companion had disappeared all too quickly into dour responsibility to her husband and, soon enough, children. When her husband had declared for the rebels, she had, out of obligation, done likewise, thus ending their association with her forever.

She fervently hoped that Emma had found sufficient time and wit to learn the truth of her new husband's philosophies and appetites. Emma's brief dalliance with the dandy who went by the unlikely—but probably fitting—name of Hazzard gave Susannah little reassurance that her friend had taken the time to fully vet his rival suitor, but she had to grant, it seemed as though fortune may have smiled upon Emma, given what she had so far said about her new husband.

That he had the force of will, and the means, to remove the entire family to safety in England spoke well of him, Susannah thought, as did the fact that he had already identified prospects for employment there. The fact that Emma had mentioned the pains that her husband had taken to ensure that his new employer was made aware of his intentions to go into the business independently as soon as his situation permitted augured further in the man's favor, in Susannah's opinion.

With the last bond to her old home in Massachusetts now severed, she felt her attachment to that place slip away, almost as palpably as if she had held a rope in her hand, and was feeling it pulled away by an anchor, the bitter end of it sliding through her fingers almost before she had a chance to take note of its passing.

She looked around her, at the grey of an autumn day in Halifax, the houses that had once felt cramped close by one another now looking as though they were simply glad for the company, the stern fort overlooking the town, and the gentle hills beyond, and for the first time, she felt that she was truly at home here.

The neighbors she had known back in Massachusetts were now mortal enemies, or else scattered by the flames of the war that those enemies had stoked. If she were to travel back to her onetime home, it would be barren and strange, a charcoaled skeleton where she once had laughed and played, unfriendly gazes from those with whom she might have otherwise shared a quick smile or gossip, and desolation in place of familiar friendships.

Here, she had the steadfast and cheerful company of Missus MacFarland, the conveniences of a modern and comfortable home, and her exhilarating and complex friendship with Colin. Too, this place had brought into her life the quiet and self-assured—if perhaps delicate—presence of her step-mother, which was no mean advantage.

Even the encroaching chill that caused her to pull her comfortable coat closer about herself, lest she arrive home chilled to the bone, that was now just another part of the familiar cycle of years for her now in this place that had, against her wishes and against long odds, become home.

Having come to this happy conclusion, over the melancholy of the news of the day, she was unprepared for the sight that greeted her as she approached her home. Huddled on the road before the house, wrapped in a torn and scorched blanket, was a pathetic figure, and when her face turned toward Susannah, she was shocked to recognize Michelle, formerly her servant and confidante, then her rival for the heart she did not even know she desired, and finally the revealer of her mutual interest in that same heart.

The expression in the girl's eyes was full of pleading as she stood and faced Susannah, her head bowed, with only her gaze lifted to meet Susannah's, and said, "Please, I could not think of who else I might turn to for aid in my hour of need. The American rebels have burnt my father's farm, misused me shamefully, and left none other from the homestead breathing."

After speaking, she swayed slightly and then collapsed onto the dirt, where she lay motionless while Susannah, her heart in her throat, stooped to her side and cried out at the top of her lungs, "Father! Mother! Come to my aid now, for the love of this girl's life! Help me! Help!"

Chapter 22

September the Tenth, Seventeen Seventy-Seven

My Dear Distant Sister Emma,
Your letter was quite unexpected, & full of news, both sad
& reassuring. We share in your grief for the loss of your beloved
Father, & I hope that the knowledge of our sadness alongside your
own helps in some small way to take from you the burthen of carrying
his memory. In a wholly separate breath, I will congratulate you on
your marriage to a match who sounds completely satisfactory in every
regard. I wish you every possible joy of your wedding day & of all
the days to follow. Your flight from our former happy home was both
wise & well-founded, as it seems that these American devils are,
once again, ascendant. We have here suffered a most grievous series
of attacks against the smallholders whose farms happen through sheer
misfortune to lie close by the shoreline. This set of attacks has led us
to a most curious & uncomfortable circumstance at present, which I
shall now attempt to relate in some sensible fashion. I must assume
that my last letter, addressed as it was to your former home, has not
reached you, nor shall it ever, so I will attempt to retell some of what
that missive might have informed you of. Mister Colin McRae &
I have come to an understanding that he may not pursue my hand
until a decent period has passed since the termination of his suit
for our former serving-girl, Miss Michelle Stayton, whose father

held a farmstead well outside of town, along the shore. You may be anticipating where the thread of my narrative will lead, but you cannot possibly guess at what this coincidence of situation & events has brought to pass. Last week, after I had received your letter, I came home to find Miss Michelle upon our step, much abused, & bearing a tale of woe & destruction. Her family slaughtered, the livestock snatched away to feed the ravenous piratical raiders, & their baser hungers satisfied upon her innocence, she had nowhere to turn, but to our familiar household, where, indeed, despite what rivalry may be guessed at between us over the matter of Colin & his shifting loyalties of all sorts, she has found protection & healing. My mother is working tirelessly to return the girl to the bloom of her health, & my father has gone down to the government house to demand that immediate action be taken against the horrendous depredations of our tormentors. The efforts at restoring Miss Michelle to her mind & body have met with somewhat more success than the effort to ensure that no other girl shall be subjected to the like, but we hope for eventual success in both degrees. Papa is not without some influence with the government, & Mother is as skilled a healer as she is gentle, both qualities which are put sorely to the test in physicking our Miss Michelle. Her wounds are not severe, but she passes in & out of sleep like one who has suffered a blow to the head, & when she is awake, she is much of the time in a sad state of confusion, calling for her father & brothers, though they will never again answer her in this world. We are praying for her healing in all of this. No other farm has been so sorely attacked as hers, & as the despicable creatures who performed in this attack carried off even the corpses of her kin, those who wish to believe the best of our Enemies deny that they were even murthered, & claim that some lesser ill fate has befallen them. However, Miss Michelle, when she has been lucid, has told us clearly that they were clubbed until they lay lifeless, & that she was forced to keep company with their wretched remains during her own ordeal. O! These are hard times that we must endure, when no girl in these parts may feel safe unaccompanied by someone capable of seeing to her defence. Colin, for all that he once had an abiding interest in Miss Michelle, has evinced no desire to do other than to see to my continued safety, as he says that Papa & Mother will adequately see to the safety of his former intended, & tho he wishes her no ill at all, least of all the ill-fortune that has visited her, he will not visit her, both because he believes that she does not wish to see him, & because she lost his friendship through the most wicked & untrue letter that she penned for him at the termination of their suit. In any event, I should be most satisfied to see our violators here so treated as has been your Jack within his cage, providing entertainment for the crows. There is not detectible shred of human decency left in their souls, & there can be no satisfactory answer for their crimes. I am eager to see them drop at the gallows, & if I do not outwardly join them in their jig, you may be assured that I would dance in my heart upon their very graves. I must close this now, as I have tasks about the household that I must attend to, & I should like to dispatch this letter today, in case the next ship to England shall sail upon the tide. I remain, as always, without regard to what seas or frontiers shall divide us,

> *Your Sister,*
> *Susannah*

From the room where Michelle lay in her

convalescence, Susannah heard the girl cry out—another foul dream had possessed her sleeping mind, and she could not escape the terrors that lay within, any more than she had been able to escape those that had visited her farmstead the week prior.

Susannah entered the room and brought up a freshly-wrung cloth to cool the girl's brow, which had been burning with a fever in the past two days. The herbs steeped in the bucket with the cloth were soothing to Susannah's nerves, and she hoped that they would have a similar effect on the sick girl.

Quickly lifting the light blanket that protected Michelle's slight form from the air, Susannah examined the healing bruises along the girl's legs and flanks. Along the outside of one thigh, they had turned a lurid yellow-green, mottled with purple, but most of the rest had faded to the dull red of old wounds. Susannah replaced the blanket, and murmured to the girl, whether or not she could comprehend, "You are safe here. Go back to sleep."

Shaking her head sadly, she closed the door behind her and went into the kitchen. "Mother, she is little improved, though her visible injuries are fading. Is there aught further that we can do to help her through this crisis?"

Her step-mother looked up from a small pot that she was stirring slowly with a long-handled spoon, over low coals and shook her head sadly. "I have dosed her with what draughts I could readily produce, and which ought to answer for her ailments, but I know not what to make of her fever. I have examined her most closely for anything that might signify in coming to a more definite diagnosis of her illness, that follows so closely on injury."

The healer frowned, a solemn thought occurring to her. "In most cases where a violence was attended by a fever of this nature, there is some unseen injury in the patient, and for that, even modern medical knowledge of how to proceed such that the result is favorable is quite limited."

She looked Susannah in the eye, adding, "In my experience, the only party who finds advantage in such cases is the undertaker. I will not conceal from you the fact that this girl's life presently lies in the balance, and there is little that I may do, one way or another, to influence the outcome."

She looked away, frowning. "Were I an experienced doctor of natural philosophy, I might attempt a bleeding to reduce the sanguine humor which she currently exhibits in excess, but I lack either the training or the tools to conduct such a treatment adequately."

Susannah said, her concern rising, "Is there nobody in the city who has either?"

Her step-mother shook her head, saying, "The men who are learned enough to attempt the delicate procedure are all too consumed with their duties to the King's Men who protect this city from the sort of roaming monsters who undertook to destroy this girl. They have their duties, and I will discharge mine as well as I am able."

Susannah looked away to conceal the tears that welled up in her eyes. She had so long counted Michelle as her only friend in this town that it was easy enough to overlook the brief period in which the girl seemed to have absconded with Colin's affections—a man whom Susannah did not yet know for certain within herself whether she wished to pursue. To see her one-time friend suffering so was hard enough, but to receive the news that the girl might not recover was a difficult thing indeed.

Seeking escape, she said, "I should like to go out. Do you know if Papa is currently engaged in anything from which I may not interrupt him?"

Her step-mother said, "I do not believe so, no."

Susannah nodded. "I will go and ask him if he can accompany me, in that case." She stepped over and embraced her step-mother. "Thank you for your efforts on Miss Michelle's behalf, mother. I pray that they are successful."

The healer returned her step-daughter's hug. "As do we all, my dear child."

Entering the study, Susannah said, "Papa? Are you available to come with me to the mercantile? I should like to learn what news there is of the day, if you could."

Her father looked up at her, and she noticed for the first time the grey hair at his temples, as it caught the light from the window. He leaned back in his seat, stretching, and replied, "I don't see why not. The air would do me some good, help to clear my head."

They went to the front hall and each bent to lace on boots against the muddy ground. The bitter cold had passed, but had been followed by a chilly week of rain, which, though now finished, had left the roads in terrible condition. Standing, he said, with a smile, "A wrap, I think, that the chill not reach you," and lifted her woolen cloak from its hook and laid it about her shoulders.

He called out to the kitchen, "We shall be back shortly, Alma."

She called back in reply, "Enjoy your walk," and he pulled his own cloak around himself as they went outdoors. A breeze pushed low clouds quickly across the sky, and he offered his daughter his arm. She took it gratefully, and snuggled into her Papa as they began to walk.

She said, tentatively, "Papa, mother says that Miss Michelle may not recover." Her father nodded, his eyes downcast and his expression tight.

"I find myself in a state of curious confusion," she said. "There was a time when I believe that I might have been glad to see her suffer, if not so severely, then at least somewhat, and though it is wicked that I thought that way, I find now that I feel little but sympathy for her losses and for her plight."

Her father looked down at her and nodded. "I cannot say that I am surprised. Some part of your heart probably suspected that she had taken advantage of her position in our household to come to know Mister McRae, and further felt that in becoming engaged to him, she had abused some confidences you had shared with her regarding his generally good character."

She scowled, looking down at the road. "I should like to think that I am not so petty and possessive, especially in regard to a boy who was—and remains yet—no more than a friend to me and to our family."

He smiled. "And her error was in taking your words at their apparent meaning, and failing to know that you do not always say all that is in your mind." He grinned, a twinkle in his eye, and added, "No matter how much it might sometimes seem that you lack any such limitations."

She tried to glare up at him, but a smile spoiled the effect, and he continued, "Mister McRae likewise erred in believing that his political cause was worth abandoning you for, when you were so visibly smitten with him. While I do wish that it had not cost him so dear, I am satisfied that he has learned his lesson for dallying with the rebels."

Susannah stopped in the road and glared with real heat in her expression this time. "Visibly—I was never 'smitten' with that boy. I esteem his company, and enjoy conversation with him, but I have never entertained any more serious intent toward him."

Her father made a mollifying gesture with his hands, smiling. "Believe what you will about your feelings. I can only report what my eyes saw. I did not interfere, as you have been as careful a custodian of your heart as ever I could have been."

She frowned and turned back to take his arm again and resume walking beside him, replying, "Not when I permitted that awful Mister Black to convince me that he might seek my affection in earnest."

He nodded, conceding, "I was likewise deceived by Mister Black, but I detect no falsity of purpose surrounding Mister McRae. If you were to ask my opinion, he is a worthy match, but whether you are willing to consider him or not is a question I will leave to your own discretion."

She shook her head in a quick negation. "While his former intended may lie upon her deathbed under your roof, I cannot even conceive of such a thing," she said. "Even before she was attacked, I thought it a poor idea to permit him to jump so quickly from her embrace to mine." She blushed. "There has been no embrace between us, mind you. I spoke figuratively"

He laughed quietly, and said, "I take your point and applaud your perception. There is little to be lost in deferring his pursuit, as it is my guess that he is unlikely to lose interest in you so lightly a second time."

She gave him a wry look. "I did not expect that I could have so frank a discussion with my father about these matters, and even less anticipated that you would be so perceptive an observer of my situation."

He laughed again. "You underestimate the men in your life at your peril, my dear. We are not all mere oafs, grasping after half-crowns like so many dogs at a bone. We have eyes, we think about the potentialities in situations, and we recognize the effect of emotion upon our actions, as well as those of others about us."

Smiling fondly at his daughter as they arrived at the mercantile, he concluded, "You might even save yourself some anguish by consulting with your Papa on a more regular basis, even in such sensitive matters as these."

She gave him a coy smile and replied, "We shall see about that, Papa," and they entered the shop together.

Within, they learned nothing of great interest, and Mister MacFarland was not in a terribly garrulous mood, so there was little excuse to loiter. On their return walk home, though they discussed lighter topics—the weather, speculation about events in their former home-town, and prospects for victory, there finally came a point where, regardless of Susannah's reluctance to return home, they could not prolong their absence any longer.

Entering the house, Susannah's step-mother was not immediately in evidence, but when Susannah entered Miss Michelle's sickroom, she was startled to see the girl sitting upright, her eyes open, though sunken and listless with the exhaustion of her battle.

The healer looked up at her step-daughter's entry and smiled, saying, "She has been asking after you, Susannah. 'Tis a miracle that she has awoken, and yet more wondrous that she has the energy for conversation."

Susannah's father crowded into the room behind her as she approached the girl's sickbed. His eyes, too, widened in surprise as he beheld the girl alert and upright. Miss Michelle beckoned to Susannah, and she approached the girl's bedside.

In a voice quieter than ever, she said to Susannah, simply and without preamble, "I owe you my life." She closed her eyes and gathered her strength before reopening them and continuing, "I cannot repay you, but I can do this much: I apologize for interfering with Mister McRae's interest in you."

Susannah opened her mouth to object, and the girl shook her head weakly, saying, "Do not protest that there was no interest, as we both know the truth, and we likewise know that I took advantage of the break between you to impose myself upon his attentions. It was a cruel act, and I am grateful that I was given the opportunity to recant it."

Her eyes closed again, and a small smile formed on her face, as she continued to speak. "Perhaps, though it cannot compensate you for your gift to me, I may finally teach you some of the arts of the home at which I have some skill. Then, whatever you decide in regard to Mister McRae, you will be as prepared as you wish to be."

Her head lolled to one side, and she began to snore gently, her chest rising and falling with her breath as Susannah and her step-mother looked on in wonder and relief.

Chapter 23

January the First, Seventeen Seventy-Eight

My Dear Sister Susannah,
    So we begin another Year, full of hope that this shall be the one that marks the end of this terrible Conflict, that our misbehaving Colonies will be brought to heel, and that we may once again restore the blessed Peace that had once marked our happy Nation. Alas, the news does not encourage this Belief, with the French seizing this Opportunity to again stir up further Troubles against us, by acknowledging the upstart Colonists as having formed an equal Nation to our own. There is even a Rumour that they shall soon fully Declare for the Rebels, and yet again enter into a Contest of Arms against our Abus'd Nation. We may pray heartily that this unhoped-for turn of Events may not come to pass, but History informs even the most wishful Thinker that our old Enemy will find the opportunity to damage us Irresistible. I will choose the path of Optimism, however, and believe that even with the Aid of the Meddlesome French, the Colonies' vain aspirations to coequal Nationhood will be brought low before the calendar turns again. There is an Event that I am Certain will take place before the calendar turns, though, and 'tis a Happier one. I am with Child, and should Providence grant that events will proceed in their normal Course, I will this year become a Mother. I can scarcely

contain my excitement at sharing this News with you, though I will confess, also that I feel entirely Unequal to the responsibility of being a Mother and raising a child to go out into the World in the midst of these Trying Times. I should not surprise you, therefore, that I am praying with more Cause than ever for the current Troubles to have passed by the time that my Child enters my life. My husband Jonah is, of course, pleased at the thought of impending Parenthood, and has redoubled his Efforts to establish himself in this Place. His Partnership, which I believe had mentioned prior—tho my memory is greatly Imperfect even in early these days of my Pregnancy—has been most Successful, and his Employer is already making certain Arrangements, that Jonah may become a Provisioner to the Navy Shipyard in this town, and thus to the Royal Navy's men throughout the World. 'Tis curious indeed to imagine men at every Corner of the King's Domain benefiting from the fine work of his familiar Hands, and indeed, that Benefit aiding in the Conduct of this selfsame Conflict. So, in this roundabout way, he is doing what he can to ensure the Safety of his babe, as well. I apologize for the Brevity of this letter, but I find that I Tire so very easily in my Condition. I am told that many Mothers find that they regain their strength in the later Months of their pregnancies, so perhaps this is but a passing Moment. I am hopeful of good news of your House-guest and former Serving-girl, and deeply curious for news of your Progress in moving Colin's heart—or his at moving yours, as the case may be. Until I shall again have an Opportunity to read your words, I am,

> *Your English Sister,*
> *Emma*

The wind buffeted the house, making the windows

rattle in their panes and the candles leap, creating grotesque shadow plays upon the walls. Susannah shivered in spite of the warm fire that crackled in the hearth, but she focused on the task she was engaged in.

Under her uncertain hands, a ball of dough was forming, still so sticky that she could scarcely pull her fingers free, and when she did, they were covered in gooey strands. She dipped one hand into the open flour-bin and scooped up a handful, working it into the dough, willing the frustration she was feeling to settle down.

In a few more minutes' time, as she continued to work the dough, it began to pull free of her fingers—and the tabletop—and became smooth and elastic. It was still sticky to the touch, though, so she dusted it with a bit more flour, and worked that in. She lifted the ball from the table and into a wooden bowl, dusted liberally with yet more flour, and laid a cloth over it. Wiping her hands together to begin the long process of clearing all of the bits of adherent material from between her fingers—and worse, under her fingernails—she turned to her instructor expectantly.

Miss Michelle reached out from where she sat beside the table to press down on the cloth covering the bowl, and nodded at Susannah, saying in a quiet voice, "That looks to be your best bread yet. Let us see how it rises, and prepare the oven whilst we wait." Susannah accepted the praise with a graceful nod, and turned back to the hearth.

She slowly raked the embers out of the hot bread-oven with a long handled hoe, filling a hammered metal hopper built for the purpose. She poured the embers into fireplace beside the main fire, and then wetted down the end of a broom to sweep the floor of the cavity, built into the side of the fireplace. As the broom touched the hot bricks of the oven, it hissed and sizzled, and steam poured out of the opening.

Satisfied that the oven was clean enough for the bread, Susannah stepped away, mopping her brow with her hand and setting the broom beside the hearth to dry. Though the wind still howled without, and she could hear pellet-like snowflakes hitting the windowpanes, the kitchen was warm to the point of discomfort now.

The active barm she had put into the bread dough was already doing its work, and Susannah could see that the cloth covering the bowl where it rested was being lifted by the rising bread. She sat across the table from Miss Michelle to wait while the bread rose and the oven cooled to a working temperature.

Gesturing at the darkening windows, Susannah asked, "How much snow do you expect we might receive by daylight?"

The girl shrugged. "'Tis anyone's guess. The sunset was fearsome red, but that doesn't always tell you all. We shall have to wait for the morning."

Susannah sighed, nearly despairing of getting any kind of conversation out of the girl, and turned to pick up her old primer. Turning the well-thumbed pages, she came to the picture alphabet, and as she had so often in these years of conflict, she paused on the entry for K:

> *Our K I N G the good*
> *No man of blood*

The coarse woodcut illustration of the figure meant to represent the King was a dour-faced man in a crown and wig, and she gazed upon it, wondering why a leader who clearly did not seek for blood had so often found it, here in the Colonies, and upon the seas, where the French were, as feared, now threatening British shipping.

She had been pondering the question for some time when Miss Michelle spoke up, startling her from her reverie. She asked shyly, "How is it that you have learnt to read?"

Susannah looked up at the girl, replying diffidently, "My Papa ensured that I had a tutor for as long as I needed one, and she saw to my education in such matters." She closed and lifted the book. "Indeed, she is the one who gifted me with this book upon our departure from Massachusetts."

Still in a quiet and shy tone, Miss Michelle asked, "May I look at it?"

Susannah shrugged. "Certainly, why not?"

The girl held out her hand and Susannah placed the book carefully in it and watched as her former serving-girl opened the book and paged through it, avidly examining each leaf. Finally, she looked up at Susannah. "Would you—I mean to say, could you spare the time, to teach me to read?"

Again startled, Susannah took a moment before slowly answering, "Yes, Michelle, I can do that for you."

The girl gave her a grateful, modest smile and looked back down at the book, continuing to turn its pages as the wind blew and the snow fell outside.

Chapter 24

April the 5th, a. d. 1778

My Dear Sister Emma,

I give you all possible joy of your impending motherhood. I so wish that we were not separated by half the Earth at this time, as nothing would be sweeter than to help you through this time, & at the end to hold your sweet babe in my arms. Your mother must be simply overcome with joy, for her part. We have here heard no word as of yet regarding the French & what decision they may make in regard to involving themselves in our affairs, as we manage the trouble with our rebellious Colonies. You may be sure, however, that when they next suffer some internal convulsion, it will be all too easy for we English to justify likewise inserting ourselves into their internal quarrels. Thus ever are our military men kept employed. In these parts, the construction & reinforcement of Fort Howe, at Saint John, & the several fortifications around Halifax proper, as well as a veritable forest of tents, all bristling with armed men, have tended to dissuade any designs that the rebels may have upon our fair town any longer. Some of the nearby settlements have been threatened by the Indians, who are much encouraged by what traitorous invaders yet sneak around in the forests around & about, but they, too, are much impressed with the forces here assembled. You may be eager for news of Miss Michelle; I am most gratified to report that with the skilled & gentle care of my step-mother, she is recovered wholly from her ordeal, though she is quieter than ever, & has expressed a strong preference to never again be alone in the company of any man, not even Papa, & to never again live near the Sea. As all of her people were lost in the attack on their farmstead (though their corpses never found, likely carried away & disposed of at Sea by the brigands who committed these heinous crimes, to conceal their vicious acts from the eyes of a just world), & she has no other place to go, she has returned to her prior service in our household, tho that does leave matters between Colin & I at an awkward pass. He yet bears her some measure of ill will for her brutal words to him at their break, & she, of course, has little good to say about him, between his unfaithfulness to our King, & the misplaced devotion to myself, even while they were betrothed. At the same time, she has taken up again the unfinished project of teaching me the arts of the kitchen & hearth, for the purpose of making a creditable home, whether, as she says, with him or with someone else. To be completely honest, I despair at times of matters between Mister McRae & your faithful correspondent reaching anything resembling a satisfactory resolution. We are returned to our habit of passing time together—but, only when I am away from my house, where Miss Michelle's presence is repellent to him. They are both people of good hearts, despite the unintended hurt that they once did me, & I have come to love them each in their own ways. Do you know, this marks the first moment at which I have used that word in regard to Mister McRae, & I am forced to confess that it does cause a thrill of the undiscovered future to pass down my spine. 'Tis a curious thing, but one upon which

I will not remark further, until I have been granted the time to understand its meaning. In keeping with our restored situation, Papa has sought out the return of my old tutor, Master Grant, for the purpose of finishing my neglected lessons. There was some delay in securing his services anew, as he had taken a position as a sort of clerk at the government house, but that engagement found its completion, & he was once again available. Papa is quite pleased at his return, tho I confess that I find the time with him unutterably dull, particularly when the sun is shining & the air is sweet with the promise of spring. La, how nearly poetical I wax! Perhaps the lessons are not so bad a thing, after all. I look forward to what news you can give of your condition, & your progress toward being delivered of your babe. Again, such joy leaps in my heart at the thought of you with a child in arms. Until I shall again receive news from you, I remain,

> *Your Faithful Sister,*
> *Susannah*

The air was indeed sweet, as the leaves had burst forth from the dormant trees, and flowers perfumed the air from every unused patch of soil all about the town. The panic of the past season had passed with the strengthening of the garrisons throughout the region, and increased patrols by ship of the shores, and so Susannah set off unaccompanied to hear the news and gossip at the mercantile.

There, she found Mister MacFarland deep in discussion with a grizzled old farmer, Mister Barnes, whom she knew but slightly, but whose coarse manners she remembered well enough. As she entered, she heard him conclude a comment, "'Tis a good thing indeed for us here that good old Governor Lawrence had the foresight to send the Frenchies on their way, else we would now be needing to watch our every movement through this country."

Susannah came to stand at the other end of the counter from the farmer, not quite far enough away that the reek of his hard labors could not penetrate her senses, and MacFarland gave her a quick smile as she took up a position there and quietly listened to the two men banter back and forth.

The shopkeeper nodded slowly in agreement. "Though there was no possibility that he possessed a foreknowledge of what was to come to pass here, it would be most dangerous to have a large population among us here, whose loyalty to their former King in Paris might still tug at them and shape their actions."

The farmer, his mouth pinched in disapproval, said, "I am uncomfortable enough with what few were suffered to stay, and not rounded up to return to France before their daft King Louis concocted this latest plan to confound our management."

Mister MacFarland tilted his head in thought as he considered how to respond to this comment, and he finally replied diplomatically, "Those few who were permitted to maintain themselves on their old lands swore their allegiance to the British Crown, and some of those families are solid customers, and have some good people in them."

The farmer scowled and looked for a moment as though he might spit, but then he said, reluctantly, "You're not entirely wrong, I've had occasion to do one sort of business or another with some of them, and when I can understand what they are after, they are decent enough people, I suppose 'tis true. It just raises my hackles to know that we have old French citizens living among us, even as we now go to war against their old country."

Susannah gasped at this, and despite herself, interjected, "The French have entered the war in earnest?"

Mister MacFarland turned to her and nodded solemnly. "Aye, and 'tis said they have ordered troops assembled to come directly to the Colonies in support of the rebels' cause."

She shook her head sadly. "My friend in England warned me that it was expected that the French might soon openly declare for the Americans, but I believe that all had hoped that they might confine their interference to a matter of merely contributing materiel and money to their cause, with an aim to disrupting British holdings here."

The farmer looked at her, and his wandering gaze brought a flush to her cheeks before he said, "When you have treated with the French for as long as I have, you come to expect that anything you might dream them capable of, they will exceed, and often by a very large degree."

Glancing back at Mister MacFarland, he uttered a sharp bark of sardonic laughter and said, "I think it must be some characteristic of their poncy language, that addles their minds and keeps them from being able to hold a loyal thought for any time."

He gathered himself together and picked up his packages from the counter. "I'll beg your pardon now, but I have work that I need to attend to before the sun goes down, so I had best be on my way back." He ducked his head in a caricature of good manners and said, "'Twas good to see you again, Miss Susannah. Tell your pap that I am looking for my best crop yet, so long as the weather holds this whole season through."

She acknowledged his half-bow with more grace than with which it had been delivered, and said, "I shall be certain to do so, Mister Barnes."

After the old farmer had closed the door behind himself, Susannah took a deep breath and exhaled sharply, as though to cleanse herself of his presence. She said, as the shopkeeper's expression revealed that he understood her reaction completely, "Well, Mister MacFarland, aside from this ill news of the war, is there any other intelligence of import to us here?"

He shrugged slightly and replied, "Aye, but it is mostly related to the movement of ships about the harbor and provisioning for embarkation of armies for their dispatch to distant battlefields. None of that has much impact on your affairs, though your Papa may be slightly affected, one way or another."

Susannah nodded in agreement. "I will not trouble you for the details of these matters, as I will have no hope of faithfully relaying them to Papa, and he would likely rather gain more information from you himself."

He smiled at her self-deprecation and said, "There was one other matter which you might find of some passing interest. Your especial friend, Colin McRae, was in yesterday, and informed the Missus that he had volunteered to join in the army, and but awaited a response from the commander with whom he made his application."

Chapter 25

Thirteenth May, anno domini 1778

My Dear Sister Emma,
I could not delay my letter to you to await your answer to my last, for there is much that I must relate, if only to unburthen my heart to the paper, which has no particular point of view in the matters which cloud my mind in these fretful days. My foolish & impetuous friend Colin, in what he tells me is a gesture meant to demonstrate to me that his heart can be constant in the pursuit of his goal, having renounced his interest in aiding the Rebel cause, has now joined the Militia in support of His Majesty's troops. He had desired service with the Royal Militia, but I confess some relief that he was refused that posting, due to the suspicion that his conversion from Whiggish thought may not be complete. Those volunteers are being misused as humble colliers at Cape Breton, to supply coal for heating the tents of the regular regiments raised from British soil, & so it was some measure of comfort that Colin was instead assigned to the Fencibles, where he now forms a portion of the defence of our own hearths & homes, & will not be likely at all to be sent to flirt with disease, dismemberment, & death in those selfsame Colonies that you & I have both quit for our safety. He is most eager for his coat of green & buff, though such military airs charm me not. He did not seek my counsel before

undertaking this design, & had he but done so, I would have given him cause enough to choose a different method to try to prove his fealty to the country I love. Alas, 'tis done, though. This matter has caused me to give great thought to the matter of how things lie between Mister McRae & myself, in truth. Am I utterly wicked for having delayed his suit for me with such steadfastness? My reasons for doing so seemed sound—I thought it best to assure myself (and him, if the truth be known) that his desire for my hand was not a mere second-best choice, once he was spurned my Miss Michelle. I furthermore sought to be certain that his suit for her would not rekindle, given the slightest puff of air from the bellows of chance & fortune. The latter concern was entirely misplaced, & as for the former, on the few occasions that I have broached the subject in conversation with Miss Michelle, 'tis clear enough that between the two of us, I was never his second-best choice, which was part of what led her to break with him so forcefully. Now, however, with his rash decision to enter the martial profession, I have a new reason to misdoubt that he & I will ever make a match under Heaven. I ask you, if his intent to pursuit me were sincere, would he not grant me the courtesy of a consultation before making so substantial a commitment, with a price that may indeed rise so far as to claim his life itself? I either have no stake in these matters, because we are never to enter into a partnership, or else I am intimately affected by them, & the decision should have been made under my advice, & with my knowledge beforehand. I am lost in the two competing thoughts, & I eagerly await your point of view in these matters. I should be most ashamed of myself, however, if I failed to both inquire after & wish the best for your

health & progress in your pregnancy. 'Tis a miracle that I may someday experience for myself, tho these late events give me despair over what circumstances must obtain for that happy condition to develop. Despite my unhumble pre-occupation in this letter with matters on this side of the Ocean, I remain constant as—
  Your Devoted Sister,
  Susannah

The afternoon was already relatively warm for a late spring day, but the task to which Susannah and Michelle bent their efforts promised to make them both drip with sweat, even without the sun's help.

Susannah, in her continuing education under her former serving girl's tutelage, had asked innocently how butter might be made. She had a vague idea that it involved skimmed cream, left for some days to ripen properly, then dashed about in a purpose-build drum, but Michelle soon disabused her of the notion that it was so simple.

"First of all," the girl said pedantically, "there are differing schools of thought as to whether 'tis necessary to skim the cream off of the milk, or better to use the whole of the milk. Back in England, I was taught to use only the cream, and to leave it for at least three days in the churn, that it might develop the best flavor, which is to say, a little bit off sweet." She paused at the front step of the house to set down her load, and mopped her brow.

The girls both carried buckets of fresh milk, purchased from a farm just north of the town proper. The road was relatively smooth this late in the spring, having been well-used since the mud of the thaw had dried sufficiently, but the buckets were quite heavy, and they were walking with a slow and deliberate pace down the road, lest they spill and waste their cargo.

"In these, parts, however, the custom is to use the milk as fresh as possible, and to not separate the cream at all, but to use the entirety of the milk in the butter. It gives a sweeter flavor, but 'tis more labor, as you must dash about a much greater volume of liquid at the early stages. As we are both able to work the churn, we are in no danger of exhausting ourselves before the butter may form, so we will observe the local custom." She opened the door and carried her bucket inside, with Susannah following her to the churn, borrowed for the day from Missus MacFarland.

Once inside, they went directly to the kitchen, and Michelle lifted her bucket to pour the milk directly into the top of the churn, having had the foresight, after giving it a good rinse with fresh seawater that morning, to leave the lid off to one side. As she finished with her bucket, she motioned Susannah over to make her contribution to the churn. The sweet aroma of the fresh milk filled the kitchen, and the girls smiled at each other.

As Susannah put her bucket down, Michelle picked up the top of the churn and turned it upside-down, showing it to her student. "These blades, fashioned into a cross shape and cut so that they will pass easily through the milk, will dash it about within the churn, and in time, cause the butter to form, so long as all else is proper."

Susannah gave the girl an alarmed look. "All else must be proper? In what sense do you mean?"

Michelle gave a little shrug. "The butter does not always consent to form, no matter how vigorously 'tis dashed, or how carefully tended. My Gramma would set a needle upon the top of the churn for a hundred-count before she began to work it, and she used to tell me that by faithfully following this practice, the butter had never failed her. Mama always said that this was just old superstition, but sometimes when I came to look for my needle after she had made butter, she had to fetch it for me."

She smiled at Susannah, her eyes brimming at the sweet memory of her lost family. "The old ways were hard to let go, even in a new land, I suppose. I have never noted any particular variation in my luck on observing the needle count or not."

Swiping her sleeve across her eyes, she lifted the top of the churn up and set the blades down into the milk, fitting the lid carefully into the top. She said, "You will want to be certain that the lid is well in place. I failed to take that precaution once, and the whole thing fell over when I commenced to churning—a full bucket of cream, saved over a week of milking." She smiled ruefully at the recollection, and then settled onto the bench before the churn, tilting and rolling the heavy thing into place between her knees.

"And now, the work begins." She started working the handle to the paddle up and down, in a regular rhythm. After a minute or so, she began singing in a low voice.

> *"Come butter come*
> *Come butter come*
> *Peter stands at the gate*
> *Waiting for a buttered cake."*

She smiled shyly and said, "'Tis but a coincidence

that Master Grant's given name is Peter, I suppose, but if he ever were to stand at the gate for me, I should be most glad to give him a nice buttered cake." Susannah gave her a look of surprise and the girl blushed and hid her face, though her rhythm never faltered.

Susannah asked, amazed, "You have designs on the tutor?"

Michelle giggled lightly and said, "I believe that he may even have designs upon me, if only he could screw his courage up sufficiently to speak to me of matters other than Latin and sums. Have you never noticed that when I pass through the room as you take your lessons, he cannot look away from me?"

Susannah, the expression on her face still reflecting wonder, said, "I have missed it entirely. I would have thought him wholly unmoved by female charms, so little has he evinced interest in me." She half-frowned, feigning irritation, then grinned widely. "I guess it was just that my particular charms failed to pique his interest, whereas your qualities he finds more to his liking."

Nodding and continuing to grin, she said, "I wish you all the joy possible of your attempt to bring him to profess his desire to know you beyond casual acquaintance." She pointed at the handle of the churn. "Shall I take my turn at it?"

Michelle pushed the paddle to the bottom of the churn and stood. "By all means, please do take your place before this device of torture. It feels as though the butter is beginning to form within, though we shall need to continue to work it until we may be certain. After you have had your fill of the work, we will check our progress within."

Susannah nodded, and sat down, mimicking

Michelle's pose as well as she could. She took the handle and lifted it, but as she attempted to drive it downward, it started to tilt to one side, scraping against the guide-hole in the lid and nearly upsetting the whole affair.

Michelle, stifling a laugh, said, "I forgot to warn you of that. You must to the extent possible direct the handle straight downward. It takes some practice, and you'll likely be quite sore on the morrow from the stiff motion it requires."

Susannah fixed the handle with a stern glare and lifted the paddle upward again. This time, as she pressed down, she paid more attention to guiding it, and it plunged smoothly through the lid. She repeated the motion a few times, and quickly discovered the truth of Michelle's warning.

"I can feel already where I will be fatigued in the morning," she said, smiling at the other girl. The handle scraped again when she glanced away, and she had to return her focus to guiding it smoothly through its rise and fall. She was just becoming accustomed to the repetition when the front door swung open and her father entered, his shoulders low and his countenance grim.

She paused in her efforts as he entered the kitchen and asked, "What is the matter, Papa?"

He sighed deeply, shaking his head with an expression of deep regret and said, "I have just had word confirming an event that I had feared to tell you of while it was but a possibility."

He looked her steadily in the eye as fear clutched at her heart at his serious demeanor. "Some months ago, I received word that Roger Black had escaped from the prison in England whither he was sent by our court here. Today, I heard conclusive testimony that he has returned to these shores, and has been seen in this town, and he is said to be anything but grateful that his life was spared."

Chapter 26

July the Twenty-9th, 1778

My Dear Sister,
I write with the Satisfaction of having in the past fortnight made you into an Aunt. My Geoffrey Paul lies, Sleeping for this moment, in his cradle nearby, and I am Overjoyed to report that we are both in the absolute Bloom of good Health. He is a Miracle beyond any I might have Anticipated, and my Loving Husband dotes upon him nearly as much as do I. After all of the wicked Stories told to me by women of my Acquaintance about the Miseries that they endured in the course of their Pregnancies and at on the occasion of the Births of their children, I was not at all Prepared for the Ease with which Geoff entered this world. I Laboured through the Evening of the 17th July, under the kind Guidance and Assistance of a fine Midwife who came Highly Recommended by Jonah's Partner in business, and just after the stroke of the Midnight following, dear Geoff squalled his first as he was laid upon my Breast. I hope I do not shock in speaking so plainly, my Sister, but the time will doubtless come when you will write Likewise to me of your Experiences. In that same Vein, I should be Proud indeed if my Jonah should find a way to be of Greater Service to our King and Country, as your Friend Mister McRae has done. I do understand your Upset, but I beg of you to Think upon it in the following Light:

He has now sworn an Oath, second only to that which he wishes to Swear to you under the good Offices of a Priest, by which he has promised to place himself in Harm's way to keep you safe from whatever Threats may appear. Having been Denied for the time Being the right to seek the more Personal pledge to your safety and Security, he clearly felt that this Greater service was the only Path open to him to provide you the Protection that he wished of Offer. I was not wholly Convinced before I read of this latest Decision of his that he was a man of sufficient Quality to be worthy of the Hand and heart of my Sister, but I am wholly in favour of his Suit in this Knowledge. I encourage you in all possible Urgency to tell me that you have been Persuaded by my Plea, and that you have Assented to his Courtship. Geoff is stirring, and so I must quickly Conclude this, but I do Aspire to hear your Reply by the earliest possible Means. I remain,

> *Your Devoted Sister,*
> *Emma*

Susannah put the letter aside and frowned deeply. She was both overjoyed for her friend, but simultaneously annoyed at her for having taken so strong a position on the question of what to do about Colin. It did not help that Michelle and Peter had just announced their engagement, leaving Susannah feeling like a spinster—a thought she did not give voice to, for fear of causing her step-mother any unmeant offense.

Michelle did not seem to want to speak of anything at all but how clever Peter was, or how learned, and when she could be torn away from that as a subject of conversation, she was of scarcely any use in instructing Susannah in the kitchen anyway, as she would constantly be interjecting comments about how Peter liked his pies formed, or what an amazing appetite he had for her good boiled puddings, or what a wonderful lot of her bread he could consume at a sitting.

Indeed, their engagement seemed to agree with him, as he had visibly put on weight since Michelle had finally prompted him to begin courting her, resorting to an ever more dizzyingly elaborate series of dinners, once Susannah's father had been prevailed upon to invite the tutor to stay after lessons to dine with the family.

As their employer, Susannah's father was both approving and generally entertained by the burgeoning romance sparked under his roof. He appreciated the diversion, as his days were filled with urgent meetings at the government house, trying to get some action taken against Mister Black, who had, for a while, seemed determined to create for himself the role of being the personal nemesis of his former partner. Susannah had heard him through the walls, speaking in low, urgent tones with her step-mother late the previous night.

"My dear, I must confess to you that I have been concealing from you a pattern of violations committed by Mister Black with the evident aim of bringing me low."

"First, a warehouse filled nearly to the rafters with goods just off the ship from the West Indies was fired, which would have resulted in the destruction of a vast quantity of expensive goods held there in my favor. We were fortunate indeed that the building was erected in haste, and that the builders had been forced to resort to the use of green-wood in its construction as a result. An older building might well have gone up all at once, denying the firemen the ability to extinguish the flames before they consumed the entire stock. Even so, they had to be assisted by squad of soldiers mustered to the effort."

He sighed, and his wife murmured, "But why do you place this incident at the feet of your former partner?"

"A figure answering to his description was seen fleeing the scene of the fire, and there was evidence found, too, that the blaze was deliberately set."

"I see," she replied. "But how does this form the basis of a larger effort against you?"

Susannah could hear her father pause, weighing his thoughts before he answered. "When I secured that pair of fine hounds, I told you that I was merely taking them as a favor to a friend in town. What I did not reveal to you was that it was in response to a series of petty thefts, both from the trade goods that were passing through my hands, and, more distressing, from the outbuildings about the house."

Susannah heard her step-mother gasp, "Is that where my garden-tools went?"

"Indeed, and what's more, I received intelligence that Black had sold goods that corresponded exactly to some of what had been pilfered from my stock. There is no doubt in my mind that he is deliberately targeting this family, perhaps as some form of vengeance for having brought him to justice."

He continued, "My friend urged the dogs on me on the basis of their reputation as the fiercest guardians in all the town. It was not merely out of deference to your objections against my acquisition of the animals that I picketed one on the grounds of our home and have regularly let the other to roam the warehouse at night. I am happy to report that I have noted no further thefts since that time. Black appears to have given up the effort, and the last I heard of him, he was evading the authorities by living rough in the forests behind town."

"I am gratified at your efforts on behalf of our family's security," she said. "Why are you revealing this to me now?"

"These matters will become public on the morrow, as I have prevailed upon the government to place a price upon his head for his many crimes. There is liable to be a fair amount of talk about the town, and I wished to be the one to tell you of the threat that has been now abated by this action."

Susannah could almost hear the frown on her step-mother's face as she replied, "I see. And would it not have been kinder for you to have shared this burthen with your spouse, as commanded by our vows?"

Her father replied, chagrined, "Yes. I sorely regret having kept any of this from you. I did not wish to worry you over matters that, at first, seemed to pertain only to my business, and then which I believed I had in hand."

After a long moments, Susannah heard her step-mother sigh and say, "Fine. In the future, however, I should like for you to tell me what is troubling you, my husband. Do not think that your worry has been gone unnoticed, though I believed that it was merely the normal concerns attendant to your trade."

"Done, my dear. Done. And I do apologize for keeping this from you."

Susannah had rolled over and tried to set aside the implications of the conversation as she sought sleep. Eventually, she had drifted off, though her dreams were haunted with images of Black's handsome face, twisted into expressions of rage and hatred, and she did not rest well that night at all.

Susannah sighed. The diversion of going into town and visiting the mercantile, where she had found the letter awaiting her, had now been exhausted. She put the letter away in the larger box she had recently secured for the purpose and rose to face the day of chores that awaited her.

The afternoon had turned grey and drizzly, and she was not thrilled about having to go out to fetch wood from the shed, but the stack by the hearth was low, and dinner yet to be cooked. She took her time putting on her boots, frowning at the prospect of needing to clean them after stepping out into the mud of the path to the shed. There was nothing for it, though, so she took up the leather wood-carrier and went out into the dreariness.

As she approached the shed, she saw that the dog her father had acquired lay within, staying out of the wet—not that she blamed the beast for avoiding it. She stepped inside and puzzled for a moment that the animal did not look up at her, and was then startled to note that a pool of blood spread out from under it.

As she began to back away from the dog's corpse, she was grabbed from behind, and felt a cold line of steel at her throat as a voice of pure menace hissed into her ear, "You're coming with me, little girl, and if you make any sound at all, I'll do you like I did the dog."

Chapter 27

As she trudged along before her captor, Susannah's mind was frozen with the terror that ran through her veins like ice water. What fate awaited her? How long would it take her step-mother to notice that she had not returned with the wood?

She had not yet gotten a good look at the face of the man who wielded the blade, now pressed against her back, but she had no doubt that it was Black, come now to exact an even more painful revenge upon the man he had apparently decided to destroy.

He had guided her immediately away from the house and into a field grown high with wheat. In the grey of the drizzle, she knew that they were already invisible to anyone who wasn't directly seeking them—and even if they were to be pursued, it would take great fortune to discover where they were.

They came to the edge of the wheat field, and the man behind her paused for a moment, as if getting his bearings, and then pushed her, roughly to the left, into the woods. She stumbled slightly, but quickly regained her footing. In the process, though, she turned enough to catch sight of her captor's face, and it took her a moment to recognize Mister Black, so changed was his appearance.

Where he had been clean-shaven, an unkempt beard now streamed down from his chin. His hair was likewise untrimmed and showed a complete disregard for anything approaching proper hygiene, let alone care for his appearance.

What was most shocking, though, were his eyes. Where once there had been an expression of lively intelligence, immediately notable to any who conversed with him, now there was a wildness, and an unhidden coldness. In the moment that she saw his eyes, Susannah realized that she was going to die at his hands, and though she turned away from him and went where his hand upon her shoulder urged her, she began to weep.

She wept little for herself, but mostly for the thought of those who would mourn for her, and the wasted efforts that she would leave in the wake of her death. Michelle's efforts to teach her how to tell the difference between a bread dough that was ready to rest and rise, and one which needed to be worked a bit longer. Peter's vain attempts to teach her the difference between the perfect and pluperfect tenses in Latin. Her step-mother's quiet lessons on the correct herbs to use for various ailments, and her father's constant focus on keeping her safe and his family secure.

Most of all, the promise of Colin's unanswered quest for the right to seek her hand, the extreme measure to which he had resorted to that end—all of this would be squandered when Mister Black finally decided to spill her blood into the soil of this land, so far from that of her birth. She realized, though that this foreign countryside was more than capable of performing its final duty to her of receiving her bones.

She wept for her friend Emma, whose happiness would be dimmed by the sudden cessation of correspondence, and then broken entirely by the news that must inevitably reach her. The friendly, genial company of the MacFarlands, and the casual companionship of those who gathered with her at their counter to share the news of the day.

The thought that she would become that news, that her life and errors and squandered opportunities would be dissected by those who gathered at the mercantile made her weep anew, and she stumbled again, nearly blinded by her tears.

"Watch where you place your feet, little girl," Black growled from behind her. "Wouldn't want you to break your pretty little ankle again, now would we?" His voice held the same edge of madness as had his eyes, and as he chuckled to himself behind her, she felt despair creep into her heart alongside the terror which made it leap about within her chest.

They came to a creek that flowed down the hill back toward the town, and Black pushed her uphill along its banks, away from the safety of the people there who sought him, and might soon be searching for her, as well.

As she stumbled up the hill before him, Susannah wondered what might have happened had she made different choices, if she hadn't spurned Colin's interest in her, if she had permitted him to woo her, and even win her. Might she even now be married, and joining Emma in motherhood? Instead of making her way up a muddy slope above town, could she be settling down with Colin's babe at her breast, discussing with him the events of the day, and the prospects for their future together? Instead of envying Emma her settled life, could she have shared that happy fate with her friend, and exchanged letters of sincere congratulations, rather than unwanted advice?

"Here," Black grunted from behind her, as they

approached a large boulder, split in two by some long-forgotten winter's ice, and further worked apart by a sapling which reached up hopefully toward the sun from where it emerged at the crown of the split. Behind the boulder, a rude shelter of canvas was tied over a pole which was lashed tightly to two trees. Susannah was surprised to see that the encampment was well-stocked with wood already properly split and carefully stacked, and three small casks of supplies, one of which bore a mark that she had seen upon goods in her father's warehouses.

The other two casks were marked with symbols that she decided must be those of the rebels, for they included the crown struck through, as well as crude caricatures of the King. Looking around more closely, she noticed that the encampment included the remains of a couple of tents and several firepits, before her captor spun her around to face him.

"You listen to me, little girl. I know all too well that you have your father's favor above all other things, and that your disappearance will torment him more than anything else I might do to him." The wildness in his eyes had increased by degrees, and as he reached down to shove back his sleeve, grimacing as he did so, she saw that he was missing several teeth, which gave his face an even more fearsome aspect.

He hissed, "Look at what was done to me at your father's behest, in the name of mercy, in the cause of justice." She looked down and saw the lurid scars of overlapping brands on his forearm, marking him as a convicted thief and pirate. She had heard her father say that he would be marked, so that if he ever again committed such crimes, there should be no doubt as to his fate.

It was one thing to hear the process described so drily, and quite another to see the scars on living flesh, and to imagine the process that had caused such damage. Susannah began to understand, a bit, the wildness in the man's eyes. Looking back up to his face, she said in a whisper, "Those look as though they must caused great pain."

His hand rocketed up and he slapped her full across the face, bringing the sharp taste of blood into her mouth and stars before her eyes. Her ears rung and it was all she could do to keep her feet as he shouted, "You don't know what pain is, little girl! You have never had a moment of true pain in your entire coddled, safe, swaddled little existence. You have never watched as the man who raised you to believe in the justice of the Crown swings at the end of a rope provided by the King for the purpose. You have never felt the hunger of yet another night with nothing in the larder, because you could not find work."

He spat and buried the tip of the knife in a tree, saying, more quietly, "You have never seen those around you whose connections and place in society ensured their comfort and the success of their endeavors, while you could not even eke out the barest sketch of a life without resorting to crime and fraud."

He pulled himself upright and stared her down, the madness in his eyes retreating for a moment. "I remade myself. I took what I needed from a dead man in New-York and I came to your little town in Massachusetts and presented myself as a man of substance, knowing that I must pretend it before I could be it. All who beheld me were taken in by the illusion, and I was able to begin anew."

His eyes narrowed, and the madness returned.

"Then, as I made my hard-won skills at deceiving those about me useful to my new homeland, your father became the instrument of my final victory over the Crown. His business connections allowed me to bring together a great shipment of goods for the support and comfort of the forces that have gathered to confound the King against whom I have sworn eternal warfare."

He spat again, and advanced on Susannah, forcing her to step back until her back was up against a tree. "And then, in my moment of triumph, when I was hailed as a hero to the Revolution, misfortune brought me low, and I was captured, my hard-won spoils returned to your father. And did he esteem me as a man who had bested him in a contest of wits? Did he grant me the respect of watching me hang for a capital crime against the King?"

He slammed his hand against the trunk above Susannah's head as his voice rose again to a shout. "No, he had me branded as a common criminal, a mere thief, and subjected to a most cruel and peculiar sentence, all so that he could keep his pure conscience clean."

Again he shoved back his sleeve, the angry, puckered scars held mere inches from Susannah's wide-open eyes. "He had me branded, like a common criminal, like a beast of the fields. I, who convinced him that I was his partner, whilst I robbed him blind, was thrown into a lowly prison with every villain of the land, and he suffered not at all, but thought himself virtuous for this act!"

He reared back and lifted his hand as though to strike her again, and then gasped as a quickly-spreading scarlet stain appeared upon his shirt. The echo of a distant gunshot reached Susannah's ears even before she could comprehend what she was seeing, and as her erstwhile assailant collapsed into a confused pile of awkwardly-bent limbs before her, she saw Colin standing on the ridge above the encampment, a gun at his shoulder and his face white with wrath.

Chapter 28

September the Seventh, a.d. Seventeen Seventy-Eight

My Dear Sister Emma,

I am right now overcome with emotion, in every way possible. Before I describe the causes which have left me in such a state, let me first offer you the sincerest congratulations & gratitude for making me an aunt in honour, though I can never be by blood. You did my heart more good by your lovely news than you could possible apprehend. Too, your advice regarding Colin was well-founded, as I have learned in ways that will amaze & astonish you as I here relate them. You are a true friend & sister, & I wanted to be certain to inform you of how greatly I esteem your accomplishments & decisions & advice. To explain why I am so suddenly so very given to declaring my sentiments so clearly, I should set forth the manner in which I nearly forfeited forever the ability to do so in this life. On Tuesday last, the escaped convict Mister Black apprehended me in our own wood shed & took me by force to his encampment in the forest nearby. He had been making camp there, on a site that had been established some time back by rebel forces as they plotted what evil they could perpetrate on our little town. Mister Black, acquainted as he was with their plans & their provisions, repurposed this site to his own needs, following his escape from prison in England & his passage under an assumed name back to this town. He somehow bypassed the examination of the inspectors at the port of entry here, & has been bedeviling our family since with petty attacks in the night of one variety or another. When these failed to achieve his aim of bringing low my father in vengeance for his sentence, he then designed to take me captive, for what purposes we cannot know, but which we may be assured were anything but benign. At the same time as Black held me captive, my dear Colin was engaged in a pursuit of the man, as he was wanted for having escaped prison, as well as for suspicion of several acts of larceny & vandalism against my father's property. Colin also was acquainted with the selfsame encampment, as he had passed through it during his time of flirtation with the Rebellion. He was following an intuition that the fugitive might have taken up residence there, & was as yet wholly unaware that I had been taken captive, when he came upon Mister Black in the very act of assaulting me. With a single shot from his gun—I did not even know that he owned a gun, much less that he was a practised marksman of any kind—Colin sent from this life my attacker & so demonstrated his devotion to me even more directly than you had ever intimated that he might be able to do. By his well-timed actions, I escaped more serious harm entirely, & was preserved to be able to accept with the whole of my heart his wish to court me. I blush to admit that I did kiss him in something alike a mad passion, once we had got out of vicinity of the slain madman Mister Black, but I assure you that the balance of our courtship will be conducted in accordance with the accepted practises of the matter. I have had occasion in the days following to reflect upon my unkind or thoughtless treatment at times of those who have *been good to me in many divers ways in my few years upon this Earth, & I am determined to better acquit myself in these matters in the future. To that end, let me again say how much I esteem your well-founded advice & counsel in relation to Mister McRae, & how great my joy is at the happy news you have shared with me of your life. I am eager to learn of your further news by return mail as soon as you have a moment for it. Until then, I remain,*

Your Grateful & Loving Sister,
Susannah

The rap at the door was only a trifle too eager, but Susannah was even more eager in how she sprang up to answer it. Colin stood there, resplendent in his green coat, faced in buff, and his hat tucked courteously under his arm.

He bowed slightly at the waist and asked formally, a smile twitching at the corner of his mouth, "May I enter and enjoy the company of your family for dinner, as per the invitation you had previously conveyed to me?"

She responded in kind, her smile unhidden, "You may, Corporal McRae. We have been expecting you, and all is in readiness for our meal."

He entered, and as he closed the door behind himself, she embraced him happily. "I am so very glad that you could get away from your duties for an afternoon to come and dine with us all."

He returned her embrace and then turned and hung his hat on a peg, and shrugged out of his fine jacket, hanging it also. "As am I, though I am going to leave that here, both because it is far warmer within than without, and because my sergeant will give me no peace should return to duty with soup upon my lapels."

She laughed and led him into the dining room, where candles stood ablaze upon the table, and her father, step-mother, Michelle and Peter all sat already, with expressions on their faces that ranged from approving to adoring to expectant and admiring, respectively. The table was laden with covered dishes, and the diners were closely spaced around the it.

Susannah's father rose in greeting. "I shall have to purchase a larger table," he said, bowing to Colin, who returned the courtesy before seating Susannah and taking his seat. "I should like very much for this gathering to be habitual, and this table is simply too small for us all." He smiled, and Colin smiled back at him.

"I expect, Mister Mills, that we may enjoy many meals together as a family in the future." He looked about the warm, well-appointed room. "I am grateful to be counted among those gathered here with love in our hearts for one another, and united by the bonds of loyalty and devotion to one another."

Susannah's father nodded, and then said, "Let us dispense now with the fine speeches and careful manners. There is a feast set before us, and I mean to enjoy it." The diners laughed, and the sound of dishware rattling, appreciative comments about the cooking and happy discussion carried on throughout the evening and into the night.

Observing the table as the serving-dishes were emptied and appetites sated, Susannah felt deeply at peace for the first time in years, and she carefully fixed the moment in her memory to enjoy for all the years to come.

Chapter 29

September the Twenty-Third,
Eighteen Hundred & Thirty-Two

Dear Emma,

I regret extremely to inform you that your fine letter of this Summer failed to reach your faithful Correspondent of these many years. Susannah went to join her beloved Colin & their son Richard in the blessed grove of the Hereafter on July the Seventeenth of the present year. She was comfortable at the end, surrounded in spirit by her many friends in this City & in the flesh by her adoring daughters & their Children, each of whom she recalled by name right to the end of her days. She spoke often of your devotion as a true Friend, & her chief sadness in the waning days of her life was that she had never been able to undertake the long Voyage to go & sit with you one final time. Between the demands of being a mother & a wife, & the disruptions of the two wars our Nation has had to fight against our boisterous American cousins, & then Colin's fading health & her own, there was simply never a right moment for an extended voyage. As her closest & most durable friend on this side of the vast Ocean, I can tell you with all certainty that your letters were an unfailing source of joy to her heart, & she always eagerly greeted any new arrival of shipping from your *shores, in hopes that it might carry word from you. Sad news or joyful, the notices from your pen were always welcome, & the ability to lessen her burthens by sharing them on a page bound to you was, at times, the only means of which she availed herself to brighten her darkest days. Again, I grieve anew to have to convey to you this sad news, but I am certain that you would prefer to hear it from a friendly pen. If you should wish to correspond further with me, I may be reached at the affixed address; until that happy day, I feel myself to be,*

Your Friend,

Michelle Grant

Historical Notes

The travails of the Loyalists during the American Revolution—both those who stayed amongst their rebellious neighbors, and those who fled to safety elsewhere—is little-examined in fiction, and so made for an irresistible tale to add to this collection.

The divisions that Emma and Susannah wrote about were every bit as vicious as depicted, and the behavior of the American forces was appalling at times toward the substantial number of Colonists who chose loyalty to the Crown over the uncertainties of rebellion and independence.

Nova Scotia made for a particularly fascinating setting for this novel, as it was in the midst of incredible upheaval even apart from the Revolution. Beginning decades prior to the outbreak of hostilities in Massachusetts and elsewhere, the British had pursued a policy of expelling all French speakers from the territories they had seized from France.

With the end of the French and Indian war, as it's called in American histories (though it was only one front in the global Seven Years' War), this policy accelerated, as Britain won the Canadian provinces from the French. Though they formally ended the practice in 1764, they still demanded loyalty oaths of anyone who wanted to return.

The Acadian Expulsion left broad swathes of land open for repopulation, and the British were shipping them in by the boatload. Once the Revolution began, fleeing Loyalists came to compete for land and housing with the new arrivals to North America. Disruptions in commerce and travel during the Revolution slowed the pace of the replacement of the Acadians for its duration.

The description of the "smoking" of suspected British sympathizers is based on contemporary reports of the practice, and the incident of the crime and punishment of John the Painter in Portsmouth is also from contemporary sources.

The primer that is Susannah's prized possession was in relatively wide use in the American Colonies, and facsimiles of it are available even today, providing a fascinating glimpse of the world of that time, as it was presented to children.

Acknowledgements

No work of featuring facts drawn from history is the labor of just one person; we each stand on the shoulders of our predecessors and peers, and I gratefully tip my hat to the historians whose work informed mine.

In addition, I want to thank my gifted editor, Ingrid Bevz, made many important suggestions and caught many embarrassing errors. Any that I introduced in the editing process are, of course, entirely my own.

I would also like to thank my friend and patron Tony Haber, whose request to name a character after his daughter gave me the impetus for the epistolary framework for this story. I hope that her namesake's story provides some entertainment and enlightenment to all who read it.

Thank you, as always, to my family and friends, whose support and encouragement make this inherently antisocial pursuit both possible and deeply rewarding. Thanks, too, to my readers, without whom none of this would be worth pursuing at all.

Thank You

We deeply appreciate you spending the past couple of hundred pages with the characters and events of a world long past, yet hopefully relevant today.

If you enjoyed this book, we'd deeply appreciate a kind review on your favorite bookseller's Web site or social media outlet. Word of mouth is the best way to make our authors successful, so that we can bring you even more high quality stories of bygone times.

We'd love to hear directly from you, too—feel free to reach out to us via our Facebook page, Twitter feed or Web site, and let us know what we're doing well, where we can do better, and what you'd like to see from us in the future.

Again, thank you for reading, for telling your friends about this book, for giving it as a gift or dropping off a copy in your favorite classroom or library. With your support and encouragement, we'll find even more times and places to explore together.

http://briefcandlepress.com
http://facebook.com/BriefCandlePress
@BriefCandlePr on Twitter

The Wind

A s he sank beneath the waves, Gabriel found himself becoming very calm. The water was warm, and it was quiet down here – quiet, at least, in comparison to the chaos that reigned above.

The whistling of the wind in the rigging, the desperate shouts of men struggling to make themselves heard over the storm, the crash of water against the sides of the ship, all were silenced. Gone, too, were the cracks and thuds of falling spars, the hoarse cries of surprise wrenched from the throats of men as they were swept from the decks, and the deep, muffled booms of thunder.

It was not an unbroken peace, however. Gabriel was aware of pain, both in the leg that had caught awkwardly on the railing as he went overboard, and growing in his lungs, as his breath ran out.

Calm was replaced with a growing sense of concern, even panic, and he would ever after this day remember the moment when he realized that he had a choice, a decision to make. Decades hence, he would relate to his grandchildren the moment when he realized that he had decided to live, although he'd never be able to clearly explain what had driven him to the decision.

Although a single, sharply painful kick proved that his injured leg was not fit for propelling himself, he began to kick with his good leg, and struggled toward the surface on the strength of his arms and his will.

By the time he broke the surface, his lungs burned as if he'd inhaled the smoke of burning pitch, and his first breath was more water than air, it seemed. It was enough to win him a second surfacing, and another coughing breath, and then another. He finally gained the strength to stay above water long enough to see that his ship, scarcely more than a wallowing river barge under the best of circumstances, was heeled over sharply.

He noted that its mainmast had been carried off by the force of the wind on just the sheets of rigging, and guessed that the supplies he'd helped painstakingly load and balance in the hold now laid against the starboard side, dooming her to list until she should founder and go down. As there was no prospect of rescue from that quarter, he turned his attention in the opposite direction, where he could just make out the lights of shore.

Not for the first time, he sent a blessing heavenward to his father, thanking him for forcing his eldest son to learn how to swim. "The day will come, mi hijo, when you shall have the choice of whether to sink or to swim," he'd said, and it looked to Gabriel as though this day were the one. Turning away from the sight of the sinking ship, he struck out for the shoreline illuminated by lightning, pulling himself along with his arms. As he swam, he gritted his teeth and did his best to ignore the pain of his damaged leg.

An eternity later, he cried out as he was lifted by a breaking wave, and driven heavily into the gravel of the shore. He tumbled in the surf for a few minutes, his injured leg bringing him fresh agonies each time it was bashed into something, or twisted by the swirling waves, but finally found a moment when he was deposited on relatively dry ground long enough to pull himself clear of the water entirely.

The wind, which had been devilishly rising throughout the day, seemed to be whipping itself into an even higher frenzy now, and a flash of lightning revealed the hulk of a ship – whether it was his or another he could not tell – being rolled up into the shattered embrace of a copse of live oak, a mere dozen paces from where he lay.

The sight galvanized him into action, as he realized that although he was no longer actively engaged in the process of drowning, he was far from any sort of safety. Grabbing a nearby length of broken branch, Gabriel struggled to his feet, hunching himself against the wind, and confirmed that he could move by leaning heavily on his improvised crutch.

Between savage gusts of windborne rain – or was it seawater, still? – he made his way forward, stopping to rest, stooped low against the wind, when the storm threatened to sweep him entirely off his feet. Just after a particularly ferocious gust, his crutch struck a solid impediment of some sort, and he groped in the darkness, cursing the storm for failing to provide lightning now that he needed it.

Whatever laid in his path seemed to consist of rock and was perhaps knee-high. He made his way around the end of it, and sat heavily in the lee of the obstacle, relishing the relative quiet he found there.

For the space of several deep, shaky breaths, he sat, thanking the blessed Virgin for interceding in his moment of greatest need. It was in this moment, without warning, that a heavy piece of airborne debris struck him from behind, and he fell, senseless, to the ground.

CPSIA information can be obtained
at www.ICGtesting.com
Printed in the USA
BVOW08s1011161017
497788BV00001B/61/P